SECRET IN STRATFORD:

A GHOST STORY

Secret in Stratford: A Ghost Story

Secret in Stratford: A Ghost Story is registered trademark of Ronald Fulleman and the LorRonCo company, Santa Clarita, California.

Secret in Stratford: A Ghost Story
by R. Fulleman

Cover Design by: Alex Ray

Book Layout by: Marian Oprea

Editor: S. Haughton

Distributed by: LorRonCo
Santa Clarita, California
www.LorRonCo.com

Library of Congress Control Number: 2025916949

(paperback) ISBN: 978-0-9886434-8-2

(eBook) ISBN: 978-0-9886434-9-9

Lexile 610L; RL 3.5
[1. Mystery. 2. Travel—Fiction. 3. England—Fiction. 4. Paranormal—Ghosts.
5. Family—History—Fiction.]

Secret in Stratford: A Ghost Story

R. Fulleman
LorRonCo

Other books by R. Fulleman

Ghost Stories:

Faces in the Flames: A Ghost Story

Heart of the Castle: A Ghost Story

Ron and Bob Stories

Limo for Two?

¿Limo para dos? / Limo for Two? (bilingual)

Stink Bombs

The Tattoo

*All books available in paperback and eBook formats

Table of Contents

Table of Contents

THE GHOST STORY

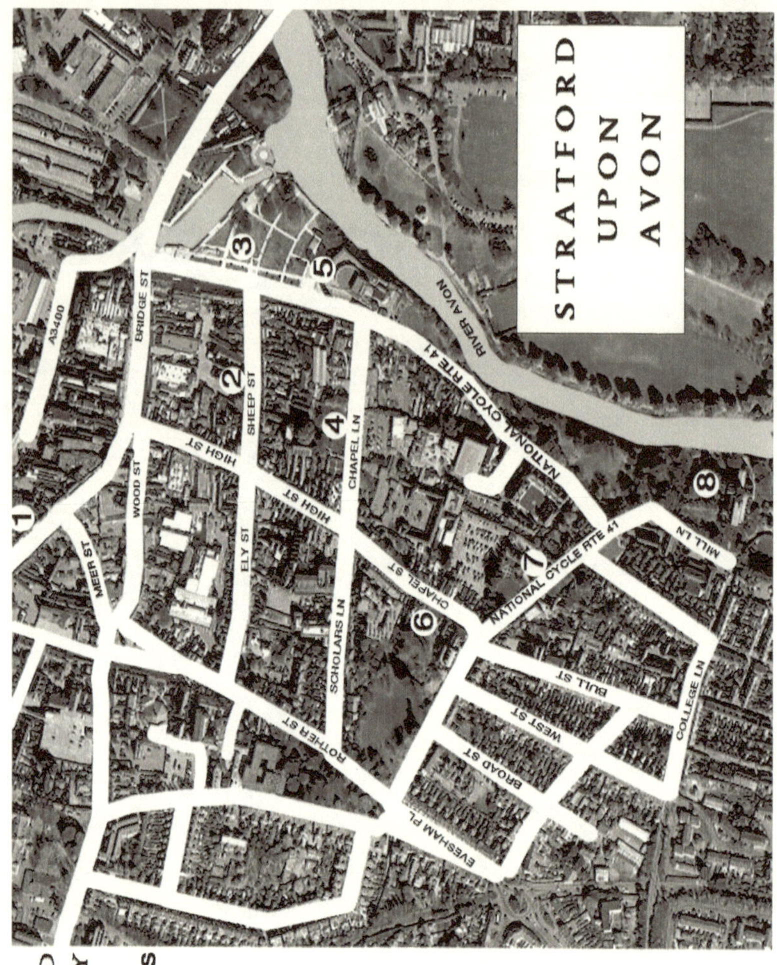

SITES RELATED IN THE STORY

1. Shakespeare's birthplace

2. Shrieve's House (aka Tutor House)

3. Swan Statue

4. Hall's Croft

5. Royal Shakespeare Theatre

6. Shakespeare Institute – University

7. New Place

8. Holy Trinity Church and graveyard

VISITING A MEMORY

Chapter 1

Ever since he barely escaped death in Transylvania, John's been doubting a lot of things. Ghost hunting was just one of them.

Now he was on a plane with his parents heading to England to meet up with Ruth. She was the British girl he fell in love with at summer school. At least, he thought it was love at the time, and he thought it was shared. Now, after months without seeing each other in person, he wasn't as sure as he'd like to be. He was glad when his mom said she wanted to go to the famous Christmas market in Stratford-upon-Avon, England. That way they could see the market and he could see Ruth.

Now, the six months since he had said goodbye after summer school seemed more like six years. He had tried to fill the long gap with phone and video calls. Neither were good ways to build the bond John was hoping for.

John's thoughts were in many places as he and his parents left Birmingham Airport Customs. John felt that he had a lot of choices to make on this trip. What if Ruth didn't feel the same way about him as he felt for her? Would they be picking up their relationship where they left off in Romania? He wasn't even sure now if the necklace he bought as a Christmas gift for Ruth was enough. And then there was his future, too. He knew he wanted to go to college. His parents wanted him to go to college. He would need to apply very soon. But where? In the U.S. or maybe in Europe? Would he maybe even want to go to college in England? He had a lot of questions, but one he needed to answer right away. Was he going to kiss her in front of their parents, or would a friendly hug be better for now?

A comment from John's mom brought him out of his deep thoughts. "John, we're counting on you to spot Ruth. Your dad and I have only seen her that one time on your video call," John's mom said. John's mom was a blond-haired woman dressed in jeans and a sweater. She carried her long black puffer coat over her arm.

John had a tall, slender build, with long dark blond hair. He looked like his mom's side of the family, though he did share his dad's facial features. John had always wondered if his hair would thin like his father's. He also hoped he wouldn't end up needing glasses like both of his parents.

"Yes, Mom," John replied. "I don't think I'll have a problem spotting her," he said with a little sass in his voice. "I just need to find her and her dad. She said they'd be here."

Before saying anything more, John saw Ruth's smiling face in the waiting crowd. Ruth's puffer coat hid her slender frame. Her knit cap hid most of her wavy black hair. It could have been easy to miss her in the crowd. It helped that she was waving both hands and jumping up and down. John scanned the crowd near Ruth. He looked for someone he guessed Ruth's dad would look like.

No one looked like they might be him. A new worry shot through John's head, *Does her dad not want to meet me and my parents?* He didn't need a new worry.

"Oh, there she is," John said, spotting her in the crowd.

"Do you see her dad?" John's dad asked.

Before John could answer, they got close enough for Ruth to run up to John. She wrapped him up in a big hug and gave him a quick kiss. *Well, that clears up one concern,* John thought to himself as he returned Ruth's big hug. A bright red blush broke out on his face.

The big grin on Ruth's face backed up Ruth's comment, "I'm so glad you're here!"

"Ahem," John's dad cleared his throat.

"Oh, yes, Ruth. This is my mom and dad," John said as he swept his hand towards them. "Tom and Jill Sadler."

"Mom, Dad, this is Ruth," John said.

"So nice to at last meet you in person," John's mom said.

"It's so nice to meet you in person, too, Mr. and Mrs. Sadler," Ruth said.

"Where's your dad?" John asked.

"Oh, sorry, I did say he would come today, didn't I? He had to work, but I can get you to your hotel," Ruth said.

"That'd be great," John's dad said, "but you can't drive, can you?"

"No, but my dad can't drive either," Ruth said with a shrug of her shoulders. "We've got great 'pub trans' here."

The words 'pub trans' took a second for John and his parents to grasp. Then, they all saw Ruth meant a bus or train. "That'd be great. We have our bags, so lead the way," John said.

John's parents were tired from the long flight. They had some concern that this young girl would be able to get them to their hotel. They were hoping the person who met them at the airport would have a car to drive them to their hotel. Stratford-Upon-Avon was almost 30 miles away. But, they often traveled down to Washington, D.C. on public transport which was about the same distance. So the train wouldn't be a problem.

"Oh," Ruth said. "I almost forgot, these are for you all." She held out a bag that was open at the top. "They're a bit bad, but they're good."

Jill Sadler looked inside the bag. There were some odd looking candies inside. John took a quick look and saw what looked like candies that had melted together a bit. The candy reminded him of some Ruth offered him and some others in Romania. Jill Sadler smiled, but leaned back. All she could say was, "Ah, thank you," but didn't take any. Jill recalled John saying that Ruth was a bit quirky. Now, she wondered how quirky this young girl would be.

Tom Sadler glanced inside the bag, put his hand inside, and brought out a gooey looking candy. He popped it into his mouth. "Hmm, that's different, but it's good. Thank you."

John reached for the candy, but stopped before he got to the bag. His hand stopped on the edge of the scarf that hung around Ruth's neck. He saw that it was the scarf he had knitted for her in Romania and he smiled. (Ruth had brought yarn but didn't know how to knit. Luckily, John knew how and finished it for her before their summer school ended.)

GETTING TO STRATFORD
Chapter 2

The train ride to Stratford took about an hour and a half. During that time, Ruth played the tour guide, pointing out things for John and his parents. The time went by quickly, but it added to a very long day of travel for John's parents.

From the train station, it was only a 10-minute walk to get to the Sadler's hotel on Chapel Street. The hotel was like so many other buildings the Sadlers saw while on their way there. The old white buildings had wooden beams on their sides, and all of them seemed twisted or bent. The buildings looked like they were built in the 1500s. It seemed that much of Stratford hadn't changed in the last 600 years.

Ruth walked them into the hotel's lobby. Mr. Sadler went up to the desk and gave them a copy of their paid receipt. The clerk's smile turned into a question for a second. He looked up at Mr. Sadler, gave a nod, and then went back to checking in the Sadlers. Tom Sadler wondered what the look was for. Too tired to ask about it now, he thought he'd ask some other time.

A minute or two later, the clerk gave Tom Sadler the room keys. Tom returned to the others who were waiting for him.

"The lift is over there," Ruth pointed out. The elevator, or lift as it's called in England, was much smaller than the Sadlers thought it would be. Only two people could fit in it at a time. It took two trips to get all their luggage up to their room on the second floor. John recalled from his trip last summer, the second floor would be the 3rd floor in the U.S. The ground floor doesn't count as the first floor in England. John had to explain that to his mother a few times before she seemed to catch on. John knew that it was the jet lag. "Why don't I leave you all to take a nap," Ruth said. "You all look a bit knackered."

"That's a good idea for you, Mom and Dad, but I'm fine. Ruth, I saw food carts on our walk here. Wanna go get a bite?" He wanted to spend the time with Ruth.

"That'd be brilliant," Ruth said, meaning that it was good. John thought it was cute how the English used different slang phrases. He got most of them, but some he still had to translate in his head. John felt he'd catch on to Ruth's British terms better after he got something to eat and some rest.

The two stopped at the front desk first so John could pick up a room key for himself. He didn't want to wake his parents when he got back. John and Ruth were out in front of the hotel in a few minutes.

"What's that smell?" John asked as his eyes got bigger. The wind had changed, and the savory smell of cooked meat filled the air. John's mouth started to water.

"We're only one street away from the booths of the Christmas Market. Let's get you something to eat," Ruth said. John nodded strongly.

John was very happy to be there with Ruth. "I missed you," he said to Ruth. He held out his hand and Ruth put her hand in his.. They walked, swinging their hands, towards the tempting smell of roasted pork.

The short walk to get to the first booths of the Christmas Market surprised John. "Wow, we're staying very close to the market. This is just what my parents wanted to see, why they came to England for Christmas," John said. "Look at all the decorations. So many Christmas trees and tinsel. It's crazy how much there is here." Christmas lights sparkled on most of the buildings they passed. Looking down the street, John could see booth after booth of handmade gifts. The smell of roasted meats and hot chocolate drinks filled the air. People were all having a good time shopping and eating. It was almost like a big party. "Oh yeah, my mom will go crazy over all this."

"I know Christmas Markets pop up in the town squares of most major cities of Europe, but I've always felt our market was filled with magic. The food certainly is," Ruth said. "Here's my fave place to buy some bangers." Ruth pointed to a booth with two men around a large grill, cooking sausage. John had to have some. Ruth ordered sausages for her and John. Both orders came with a mini loaf of bread and mustard. The sausage and bread tasted great. John was happy to see that the booth next door sold hot apple cider. He and Ruth each bought a cup and sat down at a small table.

"I'm so sorry my dad couldn't come to meet you and your parents at the airport today," Ruth said. She looked a bit sad. "I hope your parents weren't upset. He wanted to come but he got called in to help at the hospital."

"That's ok. I know my parents are just happy to be here. I know I am."

He wanted to squeeze Ruth's hand, but his hands were busy with the sausage and bread. "So, how often do you come out to this Christmas market since you live here?"

Ruth hadn't finished chewing what she had in her mouth so she could only point to her bulging cheeks. She gave John a quick little smile. Ruth gave a big swallow and then looked at John. "I come here each night that it's open."

John's face showed a look of surprise. He knew it was a charming place, but didn't think it could be that special. The thought, *who are you coming here with each night*, ran through his mind. He was a bit jealous and hoped it wasn't with some other guy.

Ruth could see the surprise on John's face. "I work here!" she quickly said. "I work at a little booth that sells old bits and bobs." She could see the tension leave John's face. She wondered what it was he had been thinking. "I'm on holiday while you're here."

"Oh, that's great," John said. "I didn't know you were working here. I thought you might be coming here with your friends, or someone. Something like that." John had to look down, acting like he was looking at his food.

"No, silly. I have friends, but we don't hang out much outside of school. I'm at home most of the time. Since it's just me and my dad, I try to help a lot at home. I'm a dodgy cook, but I do most of the cooking for us. He always lies and tells me how much he likes my cooking. I'm sure he'd cook a bit more if he were home more. He has to work a lot."

"Yeah, I get it," he said. He wasn't sure what to say, but he wanted to change the subject. "Well, I guess I'm on holiday now, too." The thought of Ruth's present in his pocket came to mind, but this wasn't the place to give her a gift.

They both sat and finished their food without saying much for a few minutes. They spent that time doing a little people watching. In Romania, it seemed like they always had something to talk about. They stood up after they finished, threw their trash in the bin, and looked for each other's hand to hold.

"I'm so glad you and your parents were able to come spend Christmas with us," Ruth said. "We surely couldn't come to the States with my dad's schedule. At least he's able to take some time off this week. We can all go into London for a day and see their Christmas markets. They're much bigger than what we have here."

John had only seen some of Stratford's market stalls, so he didn't think too much of Ruth's comment. There was nothing to compare it with back home.

Looking into Ruth's eyes, John said, "That'll be cool." He lost his train of thought. He wanted to tell Ruth how much she meant to him and how much he had missed her, maybe even give her the present. For some reason, it didn't seem like the right time to tell her all that now. Maybe it was from being tired, or maybe he just lost his nerve. He kept quiet. It would have to wait until a better time.

The two of them walked on for a few more blocks while looking at all the lights and things going on. The streets were starting to fill up. They found themselves having to weave their way through the crowds. By the time they had traveled three streets, John could feel how tired he was. He had more trouble trying to focus on what Ruth was saying. Ruth could see John needed to get some rest. She led him back to the hotel. John didn't even notice where they were heading.

"Well, here we are, back at your hotel. You're looking like you might fall asleep on your feet," Ruth said. "We'll get ice cream some other time."

As much as John would have loved to stay out later with Ruth, he knew she was right. "Can you get home okay?" he asked.

"Of course," Ruth said. "I'm only a few streets from here and it's quite safe."

John felt bad. Any other time, he would have made sure Ruth got home okay. But it was a relief that he didn't have to take Ruth home. He was so tired, he thought he'd have a tough time getting himself home and into bed.

"Thank you," John said as he wrapped his arms around Ruth, giving her a large hug.

"My pleasure," Ruth said. She gently swung him around. When he faced the front door of the hotel, she gave him a gentle push to get him started. She smiled as she saw him raise his hand in a little wave as he walked into the hotel.

THE BOY IN THE DREAM
Chapter 3

John barely remembered walking past the doorway to his parents' room. They were sound asleep. He only made it to his bed before he collapsed on it. John was so tired he didn't even bother to change out of the black t-shirt and jeans he was always known for wearing. It took all he had to take off his coat and knit cap.

John's dream was quite vivid that night. In it, he was walking down one of the streets in Stratford. It was night time, but without the Christmas market booths and decorations. The street was empty except for a small boy who seemed to be following John. The boy kept ducking into the darkness each time John turned to see what the boy was doing. Then, a girl who was a couple of years older seemed to be calling the boy.

She was telling him to stop doing something, but John couldn't make out what she was saying. As he turned back to the boy, a buzzing sound went off. The street became foggier and foggier with each buzz. At last, the street became all black. John opened his eyes to see his father reaching over to John's nightstand.

"Where's your phone, John? It's your phone that's going off. Is it in your pocket?" he asked. Tom Sadler was trying to silence John's phone, but he couldn't get to it since it was in John's pocket.

Half-awake, John reached into his pocket. By the time he was awake enough to understand where he was and why his dad was looking for his phone, the buzzing stopped. John turned the phone to his face and the lock screen opened. A message on the screen said:

RUTH: U up yet call me after u eat lunch

John smiled when he saw it was from Ruth and then looked to see that it was already 11:08 a.m.

The groggy Sadlers all sat in their beds, trying to understand how they slept so late. Jill stretched. "Wow, I didn't think I'd sleep in so long," Jill told her husband and son.

Rubbing his eyes, Tom Sadler said, "Well, it's easy to see we needed it." He put his glasses on and checked the time on his watch. "We did miss the free breakfast that comes with the room though."

John's phone buzzed again. It was a text from Ruth again

RUTH: vendors open early for lunch

"Won't be a problem, Dad," John said. "Ruth's watching out for us. There were a million street vendors last night. Sounds like they'll be open for lunch now."

"Oooh, how was it last night? Were there interesting things to buy?" John's mom asked. It surprised John and his dad, Tom, to see Jill jump up. She didn't wait for John's nod before she grabbed some clothes. Without looking back, she dashed to the bathroom to change. "Hurry up. We need to see what's out there!"

"We're in trouble now," John's dad joked. "I'm sure we're going to need to get another suitcase for the trip home."

"You may be right," John said. He relooked at the texts on his phone and then set it down to get dressed for the day. In the hurry to get ready to get lunch, the dream was forgotten.

FIRST DAY IN STRATFORD

Chapter 4

It took John and his parents only about 20 minutes before they got themselves dressed and out of their room. It didn't take his mom long before she saw a booth that was selling coffee. Next to it a booth sold pastries, so she picked that booth to get something to eat. She could barely keep her eyes from looking up and down the street while she and John's dad ate. John texted Ruth to let her know what they were doing.

JOHN: Thx 4 the wakeup call

JOHN: mom found pastry & coffee booth, eating there now

RUTH: am down the street

"Johnny, is Ruth joining us today?" Jill Sadler asked her son. John didn't think about his mom calling him Johnny since she'd done it most of his life. But what he did mind was her using his old nickname in front of his friends. He hoped she wouldn't use that name in front of Ruth.

"Yeah, Ruth texted me. She is on her way over now. I'll go look for her." John took his cup of coffee, the last scone, and walked into the street. He spun half way around before he saw Ruth coming their way. The smile from last night was still on her face. Had he a mirror, he'd have seen a smile on his face too.

Ruth followed John back to the table where his parents just finished their meal. "I don't eat scones for lunch, but I could get used to this," John's dad joked.

"Yes, they were yummy," John's mom added. "Is the rest of the town as cute as it is here?"

A look of pride spread across Ruth's face. "Yes, this time of year the town is quite special. Soooo, I know you haven't seen much of the town yet. I'd like to show you around this afternoon. Oh, and my father has asked that you all come for dinner tonight at our house. He's quite keen to meet you all."

John's parents were happy for Ruth's offer to be their guide. Who wouldn't want a local showing them the town? "Yes, that would all be wonderful," Jill Sadler said. "Of course, we'd like to bring something tonight. Is there something you'd suggest?"

"Let me think…yes, a super bake shop is not far from our house. My father loves their bread. A fresh loaf of bread would be ace," Ruth said.

Ruth's slang made Jill pause for a moment. "Great, we'll pick some up as we look around the town," Jill said.

The group got up from their table and started walking down the street. With the Christmas market going on, the streets were only open to people walking, so no cars were allowed. That made it very easy to walk in the streets.

Jill made her way next to Ruth. She said, "Of course, I'd love to see the whole Christmas market. We'd also like to see some of the Shakespeare sites. And we'd been planning to go into London to see their Christmas market too," John's mom said.

"That won't be any problem at all," Ruth said. "John and I must go to London to pick up Katie and Cam at the airport on Tuesday. But we have time before that to see Shakespeare sites."

"I must say though, I've lived here all my life, but I guess I've taken Shakespeare for granted. I believe there are a number of places linked to him here. I only know of a few so I'd suggest we all take a day tour tomorrow. They offer Shakespeare tours about the town. I'm told they're very smart on where his things are," Ruth said.

"That's a great plan," John's dad said. "Let's do that."

Ruth walked with John and his parents for a few hours, stopping at each Christmas market booth. John was right when he said his mother would love being there.

While walking around the town, they bought tickets for the Shakespeare tour. Later in the day, Ruth left John and his parents off at their hotel to rest. She went home to work on that night's dinner.

RUTH'S HOUSE AND HER DAD
Chapter 5

Ruth was glad to see her dad was home when she got there. Not only was he home, but he had started working on dinner.

"Ruthie, how did your first day go with John and his parents?" Ruth's dad asked. "Are they like you thought they would be?"

"I can't lie, I was so nervous. I'm glad it went well," Ruth said. "Yes, they were quite nice. They are looking forward to meeting you. Please, Dad, don't do any of the dad things you like to do."

"What do you mean? I'm a fine dad," Kwame said. He looked a little saddened.

"You know what I mean," Ruth said, "all the dad jokes. Please keep in mind John isn't five years old and neither am I."

"Okay, I know what you are saying. Don't make you look bad in front of John or his parents. Don't worry," he said.

Despite what her dad told her, Ruth did worry. In her mind she could see it all going wrong.

At 6:00 p.m., Ruth left home to walk John and his parents from their hotel back to her house. It wasn't far, just a few blocks, but she didn't want them to have any problems getting there. She wanted to do all she could to make the evening a success.

John and his parents were sitting in the lobby of their hotel waiting for Ruth when she got there. John had the loaf of bread that they bought at the Christmas market. It was an olive loaf. Ruth hadn't tried that kind of bread before but was looking forward to tasting it. She hoped that as much as her dad liked olives, he would love the bread too.

At first, the four of them had a hard time getting around. The crowds shopping at the market stalls filled the streets. So many people were there buying items on their Christmas gift lists. It was good the walk past the booths was short. They were glad when they were able to get away from the crowds.

Ruth's street was quiet. It was a nice change from the crowded streets they had just left. The street was lined with newer houses on both sides, all neatly spaced. They weren't the old-style houses John's mom had thought they would be. "Your street is simply lovely, Ruth. It's more on the modern side. I was thinking there might be thatched roofs and little old houses. They always call that 'English Charm' on the TV shows," Jill Sadler said.

"Yes, I have heard that," Ruth said. "I do like those old, thatched houses, but in the newer parts of the town you won't see so many of those. You will see more slate roofs than thatched ones."

"Do they still make thatched roofs?" John asked.

"Of course. They're just not so common. I believe they cost a bit more than a slate roof."

"Yeah, my mom watches all those shows where people go to buy a house in England," John said.

Before they knew it, they were down at the end of St. Gregory's Road, Ruth's street. She turned to the others and with a wave of her hand said, "Here we are."

Ruth's house was a red brick house. It stood mostly behind a red brick wall. Between the house and the wall was a garden that was full of tall bushes that could use a trim. The two large trees in the front yard had lost their leaves. Its slate tile roof sloped down from a second story level to a one-story level on the house's left side. Ruth led the Sadlers to her front door. "We'll go in this way. Mostly only the Vicar comes in through this way, but you are special guests," she said.

The front door stuck a little before it gave in and opened. "The Vicar doesn't come by too often," Ruth said with a sheepish grin on her face.

John wasn't sure what Ruth was talking about. He turned to his mom and in a low voice asked, "What's a vicar?"

"Johnny, a vicar is like a pastor, or priest," she told him.

John had to laugh to Ruth's joke, even if it was late. Before they could all get into the house, they were greeted by Ruth's dad.

"Welcome, welcome to our home. I'm Kwame Enam, Ruth's dad." Kwame looked a lot like Ruth with his dark skin and curly, black hair, though his was cut short. Like Ruth, he had friendly brown eyes and a broad smile which made the Sadlers feel most welcome. He stepped back and motioned for them to come in.

Inside the house was an open room with a sofa, a few chairs, and a TV. Part of this room had a staircase that led to the next level. John could see in the next room there was a dining table set for five places.

"It's very nice to meet you, sir," John said. He held out his hand. Kwame shook it with a strong grip. The grip was a little stronger than John had expected.

"Dad, these are John's parents, Jill and Tom Sadler. Mr. and Mrs. Sadler, this is my dad," Ruth said.

After their brief greetings, Ruth's dad asked them all to sit at the table. "The food is ready, and we should eat it while it's hot." He brought out the food. Ruth asked what she could get them to drink with their dinner. In just two minutes she brought it from their kitchen.

The meal was well cooked and tasty. John's dad joked that he'd have to stop eating or he wouldn't be able to get up from the table. As they talked, Kwame said, "So, Ruth told me you will be going to London next Tuesday. You're going to pick up Katie and Cam at the airport? I would like to go with you, and I can show you around the Christmas market there."

"That's a kind offer. Thank you very much," Tom Sadler said.

"Yes, it'd be nice to have someone who's been there with us to show us around," Jill Sadler said. "I don't want to miss a thing."

"It would be my pleasure," Kwame said. "I had planned to take a few days off while you're here for just such a thing. London is a very big place with a great many things to see. Ruthie has told me how much you want to see it all."

"I hope we won't see it all," John's dad said. "I don't think I'll be able to afford it." He looked at Jill who shook her head at his joke.

"You know you like to shop at these markets almost as much as I do," she said to him.

"Well, almost," he said. They all laughed.

After a while, the adults turned their talk to food and what they most often do for Christmas back home.

Ruth led John to the Christmas tree in the other room. From there, she pulled out a box that had a red bow on it. "I know it's not Christmas yet, but I just couldn't wait any longer. This is for you," she said. "I do hope you'll like it."

John opened the box and inside he found a knit cap. Before he could say anything, Ruth said, "I want you to know I made that all by myself." John could see the look of satisfaction on her face.

"Very nice," he said as he put the cap on. "How do I look?"

"Very handsome," Ruth said, blushing a little.

Now it was John's turn to blush. "I've been wanting to give you this since I saw you at the airport." He didn't tell her that he had to have his mom go with him to help him pick it out. He had never bought jewelry before. Now, he stepped over to his jacket and pulled out a small box from a pocket.

The box was the size of a ring box. At first Ruth wondered if he was giving her a ring, but when she opened it, she saw it was a thin, silver chain with a small heart pendant. As they hugged, she said, "I love it." She quickly put it on.

The two shared a kiss. It meant a lot to both of them. Turning towards the room, the two were glad their parents were still at the table distracted in their talks.

FACING HER DAD
Chapter 6

So far, the evening was going very well for John. His parents were getting along fine with Ruth's dad. Also, he was able to give Ruth her present. There was just one small concern in John's mind. The whole time there, John worried her dad might ask John a lot of questions about himself. After all, most dads would be protective of their daughter. John just didn't want to have any wrong answers for her dad. So, John made an effort to stay by Ruth's side most of the evening. Though, while bringing some dirty dishes to the sink, John found himself alone in the kitchen with Ruth's dad.

"So, have you thought about what you want to do after you finish high school?" Kwame first asked John.

That's just what John was dreading. He wanted Ruth's dad to think well of him. He didn't want to seem like a little kid who didn't know what to do with his life. But, in fact, he didn't know what he wanted to do with his life. He had always been content with his music and ghost hunting, but that's not a career path any girl's dad wants to hear from a guy who likes his daughter.

"Ah, well, I'm still looking into a few options, sir," John said. He was trying to think of the right thing to say. "I will be going to college," John said, not really knowing if that was true or not at this point. "I just don't know where it will be yet."

"I'm not sure if it is the same in the States as it is here. In England, it's best to apply early to any uni you plan on going to."

"Yes, sir," John said. He couldn't think of something better to say. To his relief, Ruth stepped into the kitchen just then.

"I'll help John with these dishes, dad. You should see if his parents would like any coffee," Ruth said as she heard the last bit her dad said to John.

John quickly took the dishes from Ruth's hands and turned to put them into the sink. He stayed there, rinsing them off while Ruth spoke with her dad.

"Yes, you're right, dear," Kwame gave his daughter a quick kiss on the head and left the room.

After Kwame left, Ruth said to John, "You're welcome."

"Yes, thanks!" John said. He was clearly relieved. "I hope I had all the right answers to your dad's questions. He looked like he had some more to ask," John half-joked. He was glad when Ruth didn't ask him about what her dad said. He wanted to look good to Ruth and her dad.

Both Ruth and John were glad to see their parents getting along well. Kwame talked about his job as a lab technician at the local hospital. Jill talked about her job running a small office for an architect. Tom, like so many people who worked for the U.S. government, didn't talk too much about his job. It made the rest of the evening go by quickly. Before they knew it, it was time for the Sadlers to return to their hotel. Except there was just one more thing that needed to be settled.

After standing up, Tom Sadler said, "Kwame, we'd like to repay your kindness. We'd like to invite you and Ruth to Christmas dinner with us. Of course, we'd go to the restaurant of your choice."

"Tom, that's very nice of you. Thank you. The best place for us to go to Christmas dinner would be at Chez Enam," Kwame said with a small grin.

"Anywhere you say would be fine," Tom said. Ruth gave a tiny laugh.

Jill put her hand on her husband's shoulder. "Tom, he's asked us to eat here, dear."

Tom didn't know since he didn't speak French. Jill explained to her husband that it's just a way of saying 'the house of Enam'.

"Oops. Well, we did say it would be your choice," Tom said with a little laugh in his voice.

"Sorry about that. Finding a place that would have room on such a major holiday might be a problem. They're quite likely booked by now."

"Yes, I'm sure you're right. In that case, we'd love to," Tom said and nodded his head.

"Also, please feel free to join us for church in the morning," Kwame said.

"That would be lovely," Jill Sadler said. "It'll be a great way to spend the day."

"Brilliant," said Ruth. "Sounds like a plan."

"And, while we're making plans, how about we take you to dinner in London on Tuesday," John's dad said.

Kwame nodded. "That's very kind of you. We will look forward to doing all of those things with you. Now, will you be able to find your hotel alright? It shouldn't be hard, but I'd be glad to walk you back."

"Oh, no, thank you," Tom said. "I was watching how we got here, and we've got a map on our phones. We shouldn't have any problems."

TOURING STRATFORD
Chapter 7

A brisk wind blew the next morning when John, Ruth, Jill, and Tom met for the tour of Stratford. They met at the Swan Fountain in the middle of a large park on the banks of the River Avon. The wind felt extra cold that morning. John and his parents carried the cups of hot chocolate they had bought on their way there. John brought one for Ruth too. He tried to see if Ruth was wearing the necklace he gave her, but all he could see was the large scarf she had around her neck. As they waited, a few more tourists came up and asked if it was the right place for the tour. "Yes, we do hope so," Ruth said.

It was only a minute or two later when a middle-aged woman came up to the group. She had white hair and wore a yellow puffer coat. She also carried a yellow umbrella that she would use so the group could see her as they walked. She looked over her clipboard and began telling the people about herself. "Hello. I'm Mary Watkins. I do hope you are all here for the Shakespeare tour of Stratford. If not, one or more of us is in the wrong place." This brought a few laughs. After her brief welcome, she started calling out the names on her clipboard. She checked them off until she came to the Sadlers and then she stopped. She looked up and gave them an extra long look. Her smile broadened. "Sadler? Did you know you were a bit of Shakespearean royalty around here?" she asked.

"Royalty?" Tom asked, with raised eyebrows. In fact, the Sadlers all looked at each other with doubting looks. "What do you mean?" he asked the guide.

"Hello all. Please, may I have your attention? This is a part of the tour I planned to cover later, but I believe I need to mention it now," she said to the group. "William Shakespeare was very good friends with the local baker. The baker's name was Hamnet Sadler. His wife's name was Judith Sadler. They were such good friends that William and Anne named their twin children after their friends, Hamnet and Judith. Sadly, Hamnet Shakespeare died when he was about 11 years of age. Though I will wait until later to go into that."

Ms. Watkins finished going through the names on her list. A moment later, she said, "Brilliant, we're all here. Let's be off then," and she started walking into the town. "Please keep up."

John's father hurried up to Ms. Watkins as the group walked. "I had never heard of those Sadlers before. I wonder if I am related."

"So you know, there is a genealogy shop here in town. We will be going by them on the tour. They can search your family's roots. It's common for tourists to England to seek out their family's past. I'll point them out to you when we're there."

Tom Sadler had to let that sink in a bit. For a moment or two, that was all John could think about.

John and Ruth slowed a bit which put them near the back of the group. "Well, your highness," Ruth said, giving a quick little bow. "What else will I find out about you?"

John didn't answer Ruth. He was deep in thought. He quickly came out of that trance when he tripped on a loose piece of cobblestone. Flat stones made up the streets in the old part of town instead of the tar covered roads back home. He put the thought of being linked to those Sadlers aside for a while, for his own safety.

Looking around, he noticed the look of the street they were on changed from just moments before. It was the lack of market booths that made him notice how old the buildings looked. The old buildings gave the town a story book feel.

John's parents noticed it too. Much like John, his mom had focused only on the things for sale in the booths. She missed seeing the buildings behind them. Most of the old buildings were white with brown wooden beams sticking through the outside front of the buildings. Often, the beams looked twisted or crooked.

"You will notice the buildings often have a second or third level that extends out over the street. These buildings were mostly built in the 1200s, which would make them around 800 years old. Back then, the city taxed owners by the amount of space on the ground their building used. Lower floors were made smaller to save on their taxes," Ms. Watkins said.

John said, "Those old houses look like something out of a movie."

"Well," said Ruth, "we are in England. A lot of things have happened here through the ages."

John was used to old towns, since he was from Maryland. There the oldest houses were about 300 years old. But being over twice that age here, this town made those seem almost new.

Moments later, Ms. Watkins pointed to a two-story building on the right side of the street. "This is the house in which the famous author and poet, William Shakespeare, was born. Later, his father passed the house down to him. Shakespeare's children- Susanna, Judith, and Hamnet were also born there."

To John, the wooden beams on the outside of the building looked gloomy. They looked like bones poking through a layer of old, dried skin. Also, its windows made a perfect place for people or ghosts to watch them walking past. John's shoulders shuddered with a quick jerk. Even for me, those seemed like odd things to think about, John thought.

As John was thinking about the windows, a whiff of a nasty smell met his nose. He wondered if he had just stepped in something on the street. He checked his shoes and started looking at the feet of the people near him. John glanced over at his parents. His mom was taking a picture of the building, but his dad was looking straight at him. His dad didn't appear to be smelling anything bad. But his mouth was half open and his eyes had a searching look to them. John walked over to him. "Do you smell that? Hey, are you okay, Dad?" John asked him.

"Yeah, I'm okay, but no. I just got an odd, chilly feeling, a jolt of sorts, like I shouldn't be here," his dad said. "Maybe it's a bit of jet lag. I'm still not used to being in a new time zone."

Ruth walked over and put her hand on John's shoulder. "You two all right?" she asked. "You both looked a little out of sorts there for a moment."

John said, "Sure, we're fine, but I am a little hungry. Hey, do you smell something awful?"

Ruth shook her head no.

John's dad could only shake his head in surprise. "How could you be hungry after that big breakfast this morning, and after smelling something bad?" he asked.

"Come on," John's mom called to the three. They all looked up and saw that the tour group was moving farther down the street.

As they started walking to catch up with the group, John looked back one last time. His eyes opened sharply as he saw a face in an upstairs window of Shakespeare's house. The startling part wasn't that there was someone inside, but that it looked like the boy in his dream.

"John?" Ruth called.

He turned back to look, but he could no longer see the boy there.

STRATFORD'S BAKER

Chapter 8

The tour group walked back down the same street for a block before turning right onto High Street. At the corner of High Street and Sheep Street, the guide mentioned Shakespeare's friends, the Sadlers. "As I said at the start of the tour, Shakespeare's close friends owned a bakery. It was on this corner. Sadly, the bake shop is no longer here, as you can see."

"Well, at least he didn't have far to walk for fresh bread each morning for his toast," Ruth said.

"I wonder if the baker gave him a discount on the bread," John joked.

"I suspect he would," Ruth said. "He was his friend." Ruth had no trace of a smile. Like so often, John didn't know when she was joking. John smiled and the two rushed to catch up with the group.

Further along the tour, the street name changed from High Street to Chapel Street. When it did, John's mom pointed out, "Our hotel is just down this street. I had no idea how close we were to Shakespeare's house."

"If your hotel is on Chapel Street, you are even closer to his last house, where he died. It's called New Place. Sadly, the building is no longer there. After he died it became run down. Later, it was torn down. It's only a gated garden now. We'll be walking past it straight away," Ms. Watkins said.

John's mom kept saying to John and Ruth how much she was loving the tour. "Stratford is so lovely. I've never seen anything in any other town like these old buildings. I'm so glad we came on this trip."

John's dad was going to say, "me too," but some little feeling of worry nagged at him. He didn't know what it was, so he didn't bring it up.

Strangely, John felt the same quick pang of worry. Since he was so happy to be there with Ruth, it went away as fast as it appeared. The odd smell stopped somewhere along the walk. John was glad for that.

"Thank you, Mrs. Sadler," Ruth said. "I am lucky to live here. I get the best of two worlds, modern and medieval."

The rest of the tour went as tours often do. The sights had charmed all the tourists. The two hours quickly went by, but it was a lot of walking. They all seemed to be happy to see the park where the tour had started. They knew it was also where it ended.

After the tour was over, Mrs. Sadler made sure to get her group's photo taken with their guide, Ms. Watkins. It took several tries before the young lady who offered to take the photo got a good one. "These keep getting some sort of blur over people's faces," she said. The last one had the blur between people's faces. She figured it was as good as she'd be able to get. She gave the phone back to Mrs. Sadler. *You need a new phone*, the young lady thought.

While lining up for the group photo, the smell hit John again. This odor was like when he had found a mouse outside their house. It looked like it had been dead for a few days.

He asked Ruth if she smelled anything and again, she said no. *What's with that smell?* he wondered. He was going to have to make sure he checked his shoes when he got back to the hotel.

CHRISTMAS DAY
Chapter 9

John and his parents shared a strange feeling when they awoke on Christmas morning. There were no Christmas decorations, no tree, nor presents to open. They would go to church later, like they always did, but it would be a new church in a new city that they were not used to. They all shared that strange feeling except John also had a feeling of home. He felt like he was where he should be, but he didn't know how that could be.

"Merry Christmas, John," his mom said when she saw him. She was standing in the doorway of the second room in the suite of rooms they had at the hotel. She was dressed and looked like she had something behind her back.

A moment later, John's dad came to his wife's side. He was still in pajamas and still had a bad case of bed head. "Yes, good morning, Johnny. Merry Christmas."

"Merry Christmas, Mom and Dad," John said as he sat up in bed. "Thanks for the awesome Christmas present you got me."

A confused look came on John's dad's face, "What present?"

"This trip!" John said. "It's been great. I knew it would be great, but I'm surprised at how at home I feel here. Thanks."

"Right now, it does feel good to be here," John's dad said. "Maybe just because we're all here, the whole family, though it might be something more."

John wondered, *Is that all that's making me feel so comfortable here?*

"I agree with you, Tom. Believe me, it's our pleasure," John's mom said. To John, she said, "We got you a little *extra* present." She pulled a gift from behind her and handed it to John.

The gift was wrapped, but it was easy to see that it was a book. He tore the paper off the gift and looked at its cover. "We know you're into ghosts," his dad said.

"So, we thought you might like this book on haunted places in England," his mom said.

The title of the book was *Haunted UK*. John flipped through the pages. It surprised him to see it wasn't only haunted castles or places like that. It also showed pubs and stores that were supposed to be haunted. "Cool," he said. "We'll have to keep an eye out to look for places in the book."

John got up and walked over to his suitcase. He pulled two small bags out of his suitcase and handed them to his parents. The bags were plain paper bags. His parents both laughed when they pulled out matching t-shirts. The shirts had many sayings that are used today. They all came from Shakespeare. Sayings like, "all's well that ends well," "vanish into thin air," or "eaten out of house and home."

"I love it," Jill said.

"Me too," Tom said, "but you and I better get ready if we're going to get to church on time."

"Yes, you men better get ready," Jill Sadler said.

The Sadlers got ready and had breakfast downstairs at their hotel. After that, they walked to the Holy Trinity Church to meet Ruth and her dad.

"Just to make sure, you have that necklace for Ruth, don't you?" Jill asked her son.

"Well, Ruth and I already gave each other our gifts," John said. "Neither one of us could wait so we exchanged gifts at her house the other night. I think she likes it."

"Why do you say you think she likes it," Jill Sadler said. "It's a lovely necklace."

"She said she liked it, but she's had that scarf on. I can't tell if she's wearing it or not.

"Don't try to read too much into things, John," Jill said. "You'll see soon enough. Now get ready!"

John quickly grabbed his clothes and got dressed for the day.

The Sadlers were looking forward to their stop at the Holy Trinity Church. They had heard it was lovely, and they also wanted to see Shakespeare's grave there.

The three were glad it was only going to be an eight minute walk to the church. The temperatures had dropped overnight. Also, dark clouds had come in. In Maryland, the Sadlers were used to cold weather. But on that morning, the cold was going straight through their coats. It was what John thought of as "bone-chilling cold," a feeling of cold all the way down to his bones.

Nearing the church, they stepped off the sidewalk and chose to take the footpath. The footpath went through the graveyard in a straight line towards the church. The wind blowing through the 12 linden trees along the path seemed to make a moaning sound. Thankfully, the number of people walking to church made the graveyard seem less scary. Of course, John was the first to see Ruth and her dad waiting at the church doors. As soon as he knew Ruth saw him, John was quick to point to his new hat.

The path they were on let out at the corner of the church, near its entrance. After they shook hands and exchanged Christmas greetings, they went inside. A smiling usher helped them find an open pew that would fit all five of them. They settled right in. John was relieved to see that Ruth was wearing her new necklace. The service was filled with music; a few instruments along with a choir of 12 people. John was surprised to hear some songs often sung at his church. The minister gave a sermon of hope for the coming year that Ruth's dad found extra comforting.

After the service finished, the five waited for most of the people to leave before they left their pew. "Maybe you'd like to get a better look at the church before we leave," Kwame asked John's parents.

"Yes, that would be nice. I'd like to get a look at that bust of Shakespeare," Jill said. "I saw it in a guide book." Jill seemed to lead the group as they walked up the center aisle towards the main altar. They couldn't get too close to the main altar since it was roped off. One of the two Christmas trees on either side of that area partially hid the bust of Shakespeare Jill had talked about. When Jill got closer to the wall, she could see it well enough.

The bust was a statue of Shakespeare from his waist up. His figure seemed to be looking down at his own grave and his wife's beside him. Jill couldn't help but think about how famous the man buried there is. He's still known throughout the whole world for the plays and poems he had written. Then she remembered the t-shirt that John gave her that morning and she had to smile.

"Do you think he likes being up there, looking down on his own grave?" Ruth asked John.

"I have a feeling that he'd be pleased to be there. This way he can keep an eye on things," John joked.

"Ready to go?" John's dad asked the group.

They answered yes and started going to the back of the church to leave.

From nowhere, a gust of wind hit John. It surprised him and blew the knit cap off of his head before he could grab it. Strangely, it rolled onto Shakespeare's grave.

"That's odd," Kwame said.

"Did you do that on purpose?" A man's voice asked, "Because you're not supposed to do things like that."

John turned to see the parish priest standing there, watching them.

"I didn't do it on purpose, sir," John said. "The wind blew it off." John turned a little red with embarrassment, but also a little annoyed. He had no reason to throw his hat anywhere in the church. He couldn't see why someone would think he had.

"I am sorry, I hadn't felt any wind and thought, perhaps... well, we get a lot of tourists here who want to place things on old Will's grave there. My apologies. Go ahead and just step over the rope. You can retrieve your hat, but please be quick about it," the priest said.

John gently stepped over the rope and reached for his hat. But as his foot touched the stone over the grave he seemed to lose most of the strength in his leg. He almost fell but was able to grab the hat and get his weight back on his other leg. *What was that?* John thought. He rocked his weight back and forth, testing his leg, but it was fine now. He could only shake his head.

Ruth took his arm when he rejoined the group. She had seen him almost fall and wanted to make sure he was okay. "You know it's not polite to dance on a man's grave," she joked.

He smiled and replied, "Yeah, especially when there wasn't any music. Did you feel any wind back there? I didn't feel any wind, but my hat sure did," John said.

"No, but this is a 900 year old church so there's bound to be drafts around. It is windy outside," Ruth said.

"I guess that was it," John said. The two of them joined the others who had stopped to look at some signs near the church doors.

Twenty minutes later, they arrived at Ruth and Kwame's house for Christmas dinner. They were all glad to get out of the cold wind.

TRAIN RIDE TO LONDON
Chapter 10

John's family, along with Ruth, spent the day after Christmas going to a Shakespeare play. The title of the play was *Hamlet*. It was very old, written around the year 1600. Jill Sadler had insisted that they all go to see the play. After all, they were there in Shakespeare's hometown.

They didn't say that they didn't like the play, but it seemed Jill was the only one to say that she did like it. All the others didn't understand it all. Going to the play, along with meals before and after, took up most of that day. Since the whole group was going to London the next morning, they all thought to get in early that night. They wanted to get plenty of rest for the long day ahead. Just the train ride into London would take more than two hours.

Everyone had to get up very early on that Tuesday morning to catch the train into London. The Sadlers and the Enams both decided to just grab a quick bite on the train. They didn't want to take the time to eat breakfast before getting on the train.

Ruth and her dad were happy to see all the Sadlers awake and waiting in their hotel lobby at 5:45 the next morning. Since the train would leave Stratford in less than an hour at 6:33, they needed the extra time to walk to the station. They had bought their tickets online, so they knew they would have a seat on the train.

They all sat in their train compartment, and a food trolley came by 20 minutes after they left Stratford. John couldn't help but think it also looked like something out of *Harry Potter*. He half looked for them to sell jumping chocolate frogs. Instead, he got some pastry and some coffee, like his parents. Ruth and her dad got the same thing, except they chose to have tea.

The English towns and hillsides flew past outside the windows of the train. There were patches of snow along the way, but mostly the hills looked wet and cold. They were all glad to have the hot drinks and be inside looking out.

"We have about an hour to get over to Heathrow Airport to pick up Cam and Katie," Ruth told the adults. "I just checked their flight on my phone. It looks like they're on time."

"Are you sure you don't want us to go with you to the airport?" John's mom asked.

"No, really, it should be fine," John said. "Ruth knows how to get there."

"Yes, I don't get lost as often as I used to in London," Ruth said.

John's parents laughed a little thinking Ruth was making a joke. John wasn't sure at all that she was joking, but he knew they could get there on their own.

As they rode along and talked, the train windows became steamed up. It made seeing outside hard to do. They all looked at Ruth's dad as he was talking about the Christmas market. John's attention broke when he started to smell that strong smell again. By the look on their faces, no one else seemed to notice. He glanced around and saw the steamed up windows. His eyes popped open, and he jerked a little. Now he saw six faces reflected in the fogged glass, instead of just the five passengers in his group. The sixth face was that boy again, that he had seen a few times now. He started to say something, but didn't have time. Before words could leave his mouth, the train went dark as it passed through a tunnel. John flinched a little. They all gave a cry of surprise at the sudden darkness. John's head spun back around, dreading the thought of a ghost in the dark standing next to him. The tunnel was short. The train was dark for only a second or two. When they came out on the other side, thankfully only five faces could be seen in the glass.

John was a bit flustered. He took in all the faces in front of him. His dad was looking out the window as if he had been trying to see something. "Dad, did you see something?" John asked.

"I'm not sure, Johnny. I don't know what it was, but it's gone now," Tom said. "I don't know. Maybe I nodded off for a few seconds there. We did get up pretty early this morning."

John thought to keep the vision to himself. He wasn't sure if it was just the way the glass steamed up or if he had really seen that boy. Either way, he knew he wouldn't be able to explain it. He noticed that he no longer smelled that bad smell. He was going to say something when Ruth touched his arm.

"Johnny?" Ruth asked. She had one eyebrow raised, giving John a funny look at John's dad using a nickname for him. John hadn't noticed it when his dad said Johnny, but when Ruth said it, he noticed.

John quickly turned a little red until Ruth's dad said, "Ruthie?" He knew Ruth was joking with John, so he wanted to make it an even playing field.

"Ruthie?" John said. Now it was his turn to raise an eyebrow with a "really?" look on his face.

"You kids," Jill Sadler said, shaking her head.

The group laughed a little but remained quiet the short time left in the train ride. It was 8:44 a.m. when the train pulled into the station in London.

Jill Sadler wanted to ask the teens one more time, *so you're sure you'll be okay*. Thinking about it, she could see that Ruth was very able to get around without an adult. After all, Ruth had been to London many times.

Kwame interrupted Jill's thoughts when he said, "Jill, Tom, are you ready to start your Christmas Market shopping? I want to add a few tourist sites for you today as well."

"Don't worry about us," Ruth said, to ease Jill's mind. "It may be tricky to meet up before dinner. John told me about some sights he wanted to see. And we don't know how tired Katie and Cam may be. So, where shall we meet, Dad?"

"I think the Covent Garden market would be the perfect place to meet, somewhere around 5 or 6 o'clock. There's a great deal to see there, and we can eat there as well. So, the ones who get there first can fill their time by looking around the shops," Kwame said.

"Sounds good to me," John said.

"Super," Ruth agreed.

Tom, Jill, and Kwame watched as their children entered the Tube entrance that would take them to the airport.

"Well, we're in your capable hands," Tom Sadler said to Kwame. Kwame nodded and led his two new friends through the station. Within 10 minutes, they were on their way into the heart of London. Kwame had several spots he thought to take the Sadlers.

PICKING UP CAM AND KATIE

Chapter 11

Ruth had no problem getting John and herself to the airport. They got to the airport just 30 minutes before Cam and Katie's flight arrived. They just had to wait about 20 minutes more before Cam and Katie showed up with their bags. Cam and Katie both looked good. They each had a big bag and a backpack with them when they spotted John and Ruth. Ruth almost couldn't wait until the two were out of the customs zone before running over to greet them. John was able to grab Ruth's coat to keep her from going where only passengers with tickets were allowed. Once the two were clear of that zone, John let go of the coat. Ruth ran over and gave Katie a huge hug. She had a huge hug for Cam as well.

Though it had just been days since John last saw his two best friends back home, he was happy to see them there in London.

When they were all together in Romania, talking to Ruth felt easier for him. Maybe it took some of the pressure off him to say the right things all the time.

Following Ruth's advice, they took the Tube to the Holborn Station where Katie and Cam put their bags in a locker. They could pick them up later on the way back to Stratford. After the bags were safely locked up, the four got on the Tube again heading further into the city.

While riding into the city, John pulled his *Haunted UK* book out of his backpack. "Look at this cool book my parents gave me for Christmas."

John handed the book to Katie, and she thumbed through it. "Very cool," she said.

As Katie was looking through the pages, Ruth stuck out her hand to stop her. "Oh, look," she said. "That shop in the book is on our way. Do you want to stop and see it now? I see the book says it's definitely haunted."

"Sure," Cam said. Katie nodded yes.

Two Tube stops later, the four teens found themselves leaving the station along with a lot of other riders. Katie could tell that most of the people on the Tube were shoppers. Few looked like they were going to work. There were a lot of parents with small kids and many with shopping bags. "Looks like a lot of people are trying to get after-Christmas deals," Katie said.

As they neared the shop, John started to wonder if it was a good idea to go to a haunted place. John still liked creepy things, but things seemed a little off lately and it made him second guess himself.

"Hey guys, so you really want to go there?" John asked.

"Why? I thought you were the ghost hunter among us. Wait, have you actually seen any ghosts? I don't remember you saying that you had," Katie said.

"Well no, it's been you Katie, and Ruth who have seen the ghosts so far," John said. "Even Cam's seen one."

He never did see Cam's ghost or Katie's ghosts. John only saw the effects of the ghosts. So, as long as any ghosts they saw didn't cause trouble, he was open to that.

"That's what we're here for," Katie said, "to see ghosts." Katie was into ghosts. She had found a ghost, along with Cam, back home. They found some more when they all went to Romania the past summer. Ruth had surprised the others by telling them about how common ghosts were for her growing up in Stratford. In fact, Cam was the only one of the four who didn't really want to see ghosts. He did see one from his grandpa's sunken ship. Now, he was hoping they'd just find some "ghost-free" things in the antique shop.

"I know what you mean, John. I'm ok with just seeing some cool antiques without ghosts attached. Not all the things there have to be haunted, or at least that's what I'm hoping," Cam said.

The shop was off the main road. The book came with a map. They used it to find the small streets and narrow lanes, too.

The fact that it got darker with each street off the main road was not missed by the four friends. Maybe it was because the streets became narrower, and less light could filter down, or that the clouds rolled in. In either case, it got dark enough that the stores' gas lamps were burning outside their door. John couldn't help but feel he stepped into a *Harry Potter* novel again.

Cam rubbed his arms. He hoped his goosebumps were from being tired from the trip, but John didn't have that excuse. He knew his were caused by what he was seeing. A small bell that hung just above the door rang as the door opened. Ruth and Katie led the way into the shop. John and Cam followed behind. The door shut with a loud click that made John worry that it may have locked as it shut. Since the girls walked deeper into the shop, John had no choice but to follow.

"Oh, wow," Katie said. "Look at all this cool old stuff."

"This shop is ace. I'll be coming here again," Ruth said to Katie.

The boys didn't say much; they were only mildly impressed. Most of the things just looked old. "Hello," said a voice sounding just as old. They all jumped a little when they heard it. John tried to look for the person with the voice, but at first could see no one. His eyes must have then gotten used to the darkened room. At once his eyes were drawn to an old woman sitting behind an antique display case. He wasn't sure which was older, the woman or the case.

"Oh, hello. My friend here found your store listed in this book he just got. We hoped to see what old bits and bobs you might have," Ruth said.

"Yes, you'll find I have a great many old bits and bobs. Take a look about my shop. You'll see lots."

"Are any of these items haunted?" Ruth asked very bluntly. The other teens shrunk back a little. They didn't expect Ruth to be that direct.

"Perhaps," the old woman said. Ruth's question didn't seem to surprise the old woman. "I've been told some are. But one never knows for sure, not at first."

John wondered if this strange old woman might be a ghost herself. He glanced around the store, spotting some odd looking items. He felt ill at ease and wondered if it was a mistake to come to this store. He was glad to not be there by himself.

Cam also thought it was a mistake to come into the store, but he couldn't keep Katie away from something ghostly.

The funny thing was that the teens didn't seem to notice how odd all the items were in the store. They wandered around the shop split up into two groups. Katie and Ruth ended up looking at old jewelry, hand-held mirrors, combs, and things like that.

Military items like British war medals from WWII and an old uniform caught the boys' notice. John pointed out some of the navy items to Cam. "Hey, if you see any old dog tags, don't touch them," John said with a slight chuckle.

"Don't worry, I've learned my lesson," Cam replied. "The ghost from my grandpa's ship was enough for me." He decided to move to another area of the shop.

As the boys walked around, John saw Ruth looking at an old box. It was made of wood with carvings and silver metal designs on its lid. Ruth opened it and slid her hand along its carvings. It had caught her interest, but after looking at the price tag, she set it down and moved on.

Cam surprised John when he came up behind him. Cam whispered, "I'll bet Ruth would like that. Ruth's never good at hiding what she's feeling. I'm sure she liked the box. You should surprise her with it."

"You might be right," John said. "It looks like it might be a great box to go with her new necklace. I think she would like it."

"I'll go and distract the girls. You go and look to see if you can afford it." Cam said to John.

Cam went over to the girls. He asked them to tell him their thoughts on an old item farther back in the store. While they walked to it, John went straight for the box. He looked at the price tag and could see why Ruth put it down. "The young lady quite looked like she fancied it," he heard the old woman say. He turned and found she was standing just next to him. He hadn't heard her there, so he jerked back a bit.

"Ah, yeah, I think so too," John got out.

Without looking at the price, the woman said, "And I'll even drop the price a quid or two for you."

John knew a quid was slang for British money. "That'd be great, thanks."

The woman picked up the box and walked John to the display case where she had been sitting. She pulled out an old cash box and told John it would be 20 quid. He was happy that the woman gave him a lower price than was on the price tag. He pulled out a 20 pound note and paid the woman. He unzipped his backpack. But, before he could reach for the box, the woman picked it up. She told him to open his backpack and slid it inside. "Don't give it to her until the time is right," she said. "An old woman knows these things." John zipped his pack shut.

John was sure the woman was a bit crazy, but he was glad to get the gift at a price he could better afford. When he put his backpack over his shoulders, a thought popped into his head.

How will I know when the time is right? When he turned to ask the old woman his question, he couldn't see her. He figured she must be hiding in some dark spot in the shop. That way he couldn't change his mind about buying the box. He gave up on asking the woman his question and glanced around for the others. He was anxious to get out of the store.

After much thought, Katie picked out an old hand-mirror. The old woman seemed to pop up near Katie. "So, you want to buy that?" Again, the old woman said something strange. "I think you'll like who you see in this one, dearie."

Katie hoped the old woman meant that a ghost would appear in the mirror. Even if one wouldn't, she still liked the mirror. She put the mirror in her backpack after paying for it. Then, seeing John and Cam standing by the shop's door, the girls agreed it was time to get going. They didn't want to be late meeting up with the adults.

John reached to open the door for Ruth and Katie, but when he pulled on the door, it didn't budge. For a moment he thought perhaps he needed to push, so he tried that, but the door still didn't open. The knob turned, but the door wouldn't open. "I don't know, it's just not working," he said to the others. Just then his thoughts came back to him from when he first heard the door close with a click.

"Let me give it a try," Cam said. When he tried, it still didn't open. Cam was afraid he would break the glass in the door by shaking the knob so much.

John looked to where he last left the old woman. She was now walking towards them through the rows of shelves. She was shaking her head. "It's not easy to know when to let go of the past, is it?" she asked. She reached over and turned the knob, pulling the door open with ease. Not wasting any time in leaving the eerie store and woman, the friends scurried through the open door. As they did, she said, "It's easy to get stuck ... in the past."

John looked back at her. *What did she mean by that?*, he thought. In an instant, the door was closed again. John jerked in surprise when he looked back through the glass in the door. The old woman wasn't there. All he could see was the darkness within the shop.

A shudder ran through his shoulders. He didn't waste any time in turning to get to the others.

POPPING INTO THE NATIONAL GALLERY

Chapter 12

John wasn't feeling good after the strange time he had with the old woman at the antique store. Just as John noticed his back felt a little achy, he smelled that strange smell again. It wasn't very strong, but it had taken his mind off his back. He looked around, and he asked both Ruth and Katie if they smelled something odd, but they said no. "I don't. Do you Ruth?"

"Nothing smells odd to me," she said. "Perhaps you're smelling something from the Christmas market. We're getting closer." Ruth took his hand, and all his concerns went away.

They started seeing signs for the markets as they walked. After Ruth texted her dad, she turned to the others. "They're thinking we should pick a Christmas market we want now and eat lunch there. Then, they want to meet back up with us for dinner at Covent Garden. We can all go around there before starting back to get the train to Stratford."

"That sounds good," Katie said. "Which is the best market for us to go to now?"

"We're closest to Trafalgar Square. That's been my fave 'pop-up' before so it should be good," Ruth said.

"Pop-up?" Katie asked.

"That's one of the two types of markets here in London. 'Pop-ups' are short-term. Those are only open at Christmas time. The 'permanents' are markets that are open all year, but they do decorate for Christmas," Ruth explained.

"Good to know," Cam said. "Let's go."

About 15 minutes later they arrived at Trafalgar Square. It was a huge area only open to foot traffic. In its center was a large water fountain. Huge statues of lions sat near it. The wind blew the spray of water from the fountain across the square. People were walking and sitting all around. The water must have been cold, but it looked fun. Along with selling food, stalls were still filled with holiday items, hats and gloves, and unique gift items, all for sale. Some of the gift items were made to look like old English houses, like the kind John saw in Stratford.

"Let's go get something to eat first, and then look around," Katie said. "I saw a hat I want to get for my mom, but I'm starving."

"I know John wants to go to that sausage booth," Ruth said, but John just nodded. She wasn't sure why John didn't suggest it himself though. John seemed to be rather quiet since they went to the antique shop. Katie and Cam noticed it too.

"Sounds great," Cam said. "C'mon, John." Cam could only get John to give him a "sure." Cam wanted to see what was bugging John, but he was hungry himself. *First things first*, he thought.

The lunch did wonders for everyone. They felt much better after eating something. John still seemed quiet. He wasn't his normal self. Even Ruth could see the change in him. Both Katie and Cam wanted to make the most of being in a London market place since they hadn't had time to shop much. So, she suggested they look some more. Katie wanted to go back and buy the hat she liked for her mom.

Ruth had done a lot of shopping back in Stratford, and John still looked like he didn't want to shop more, so she said they should split up from Cam and Katie. "I've got something to show John, and we can meet back up at the big Christmas tree in about 30 minutes.

"Sure, sounds good," Cam said. Katie agreed.

"John, why don't we take it easy and get away from this crowd for a bit," Ruth said. After John nodded yes, she pulled him by his arm towards the National Gallery. It is a famous art museum with some of England's most famous paintings. "It'll be calmer there," Ruth said.

Going into the building required having security people look through each bag. Ruth had a small bag, but John had the backpack with the box in it for Ruth. He let Ruth go through the checkpoint first so he could lag behind. With some luck, maybe Ruth wouldn't see what was in his bag. When he held his bag open to be checked, he turned his back as much as he could towards Ruth. He stood there for a second, waiting to be asked about the box.

"Nothing to see there, young man. Please move on," the guard said to John.

John was confused. What did he mean nothing to see? John looked into the open top of the backpack but had to stop and stare into it.

"Move along, please," the guard said again.

John peered inside the bag expecting to see the large box, but it was not there. He stood there with his mouth open. The thought hit him with some impact. "Someone stole my box!" he exclaimed. Clearly to him, someone must have removed the box from his backpack. He couldn't understand it, no one could have taken that box. *I was wearing the backpack this whole time*, he thought. *It's a big box and I would have felt it if someone took it out*. He knew he couldn't do something about it. He also knew the security person couldn't get the box back. On top of all that, he couldn't even tell Ruth about it. After all, he never told her he had bought it. He walked about 5 steps before turning to complain to Ruth, but he couldn't. He wasn't sure what to do. Then, Ruth made it even harder for him. She walked up to him, smiled, and gave him a hug. "I thought you looked like you could use that," she said. And she was right, John could use it. He stood there for a few seconds hugging Ruth.

This is nice, Ruth thought. But a second later, John took off at a fast pace towards the stairs. Ruth had thought to go inside and sit down somewhere so John could rest, but things had changed quickly. Ruth now had to hurry along to keep up with him.

"John?" She couldn't figure out why he was going so fast. *Where are we going?*, she thought. *You don't know what's here!*

SO THAT'S WHAT

HE LOOKED LIKE

Chapter 13

John stopped there on the 3rd floor, in front of a painting. The painting was of a heavy, bald man with a mustache. He stood in front of the painting and looked at it. There, Ruth caught up to John. "Why did you rush up here to stand in front of William Shakespeare?" Ruth asked.

John hadn't noticed that it was Shakespeare until she said it. He shook his head a little and said, "I'm not sure. I didn't even know it was here."

He then seemed to notice the bench behind him and started to sit down on it. Ruth sat down too. Ruth was concerned about John's behavior.

When John sat down, he felt the weight of the box shifting in his backpack. He removed the bag from his back and peeked inside. To his surprise, the box was there!

"Okay, this is crazy," he said to Ruth. He couldn't keep it to himself any longer. "I have to tell you something. I bought something at the shop this morning, but I don't want to tell you what it was."

"Yeah?" Ruth asked. She could grasp the idea that John had bought something and didn't tell her. It was him not being able to tell her what it was that confused her.

"The thing is, it was lost and now it's back. When we walked in here, it wasn't in my backpack, but now it is," he said. He opened the top of the backpack to show Ruth what was inside.

"Then, where is it?" Ruth asked. She was getting more confused about how John was acting with each new thing he was saying. She pulled the open end of the canvas bag towards her and looked inside. "Are you joking with me?" she asked.

"What? No!" While she was looking into the bag, John couldn't see anything inside of it. Things changed when she let go of the bag and looked away. John could see the box in his bag. He wasn't sure what was going on. "But it's there," he said.

"I'll look again, if you like," Ruth said. So, John held the bag open for Ruth. Ruth shook her head, "no, nothing."

John didn't know what to do. He looked at Ruth again and then down at the bag. Then, he turned his head towards the painting and looked into Shakespeare's eyes. He hoped to see an answer there, he didn't know why, but nothing there either. "I guess we'd better find Cam and Katie." *Maybe they'll have an idea,* he thought. "We'd better get going. We've got to meet my parents soon."

John put on the backpack, and the two started down the stairs to the lobby. John could feel the box bounce around inside his backpack as he walked. In the lobby, he turned to Ruth, "You didn't?"

"I didn't. Really," she said.

Wow! Is this what it's like to have a ghost? And have people think I'm nuts? he thought. "I'm going to have to talk to Cam a lot tonight, and maybe Katie, too," he said.

SHARING NEWS WITH CAM AND KATIE

Chapter 14

When they got to the huge Christmas tree in Trafalgar Square, John and Ruth could see Cam and Katie waiting for them. The two had sat down at a booth that sold chocolate. They had just finished what John guessed was a sweet treat, based on the other treats for sale there.

Looking at Cam and Katie, Ruth said, "You two look rather done in. We'd better meet up with my dad and the Sadlers. We need to see about getting you back to Stratford."

Neither Cam nor Katie could argue that. The long flight and different time zone had caught up with them. "You're right. I'm super tired. I was hoping that I'd have slept on the flight more, but that didn't happen," Cam said.

Katie said, "I slept a little more than Cam, but, yeah, I'm beat."

Ruth led the group over to a bus stop a short distance away. She read the schedule. The short wait for the bus to take them down the road to Covent Garden market made Ruth happy. The bus that stopped in front of them was a red double decker bus like in the movies. The bus had stairs going to the upper level, but Ruth knew the rest of the group was tired so they stayed on the lower one. John watched as his two friends leaned against each other and closed their eyes. They fell asleep in seconds. Ruth hated to wake the two up when the bus came to a stop only 10 minutes later. "Alright, sleepy heads. This is our stop. We'll meet up with my dad and John's parents here. You can eat something, get some energy, and we'll get back to Stratford."

"Oh, my goodness," Jill said when she saw how tired Cam and Katie looked. "You've had a long day, haven't you?"

"This isn't the best way to meet, but this is my dad, Kwame," Ruth said. Kwame shook hands with the tired teens and gave Ruth a quick hug.

"Yes, let's get them something to eat. There are some food stalls just inside the Gardens. We'll start there," Kwame said.

He led the group into a tall glass structure that looked a bit like a railroad station. Inside were many booths. The first booth they came to sold sausages. "Here, we'll get you some bangers and chips," Kwame said. He and John's dad went to get the food while all the others found some tables. Cam tried to stay awake but fell asleep sitting at the table. He didn't have time to sleep long. Five minutes later, Tom slid a paper basket with two sausages, and some french fries in front of Cam. It surprised Katie at how fast Cam woke up.

The smell of the food helped to revive all the tired teens. The food was a little greasy, but the taste of home helped them feel so much better. Kwame also brought them some tea. He knew they needed something more to help them stay awake until they could get back to Stratford.

Helping Cam and Katie get to Covent Garden and eating had taken John's mind off his backpack. He jiggled it a little bit and could feel the box shift inside. He was still confused. He wondered if he was just tired from all the changes going on, being in a new place, or if it was some ghostly thing.

They got on the Tube at the Covent Gardens station and made the short trip to the Holborn station to get Cam and Katie's bags out of storage. A little over two hours later they all were stepping off the train at the little Stratford-Upon-Avon station.

Katie said her goodbyes to Cam as she went with Ruth and her dad back to their house. Katie was staying with them during this trip. Cam was sharing a room with John in the hotel with the Sadlers, so he went off with them.

John helped out by rolling Cam's bag to their hotel. He could see Cam was exhausted. Cam was grateful that the hotel had an elevator. He just wasn't up to carrying his bag up some stairs.

In their room, Cam kicked off his shoes and collapsed onto his bed without changing his clothes. John had other things he needed to do.

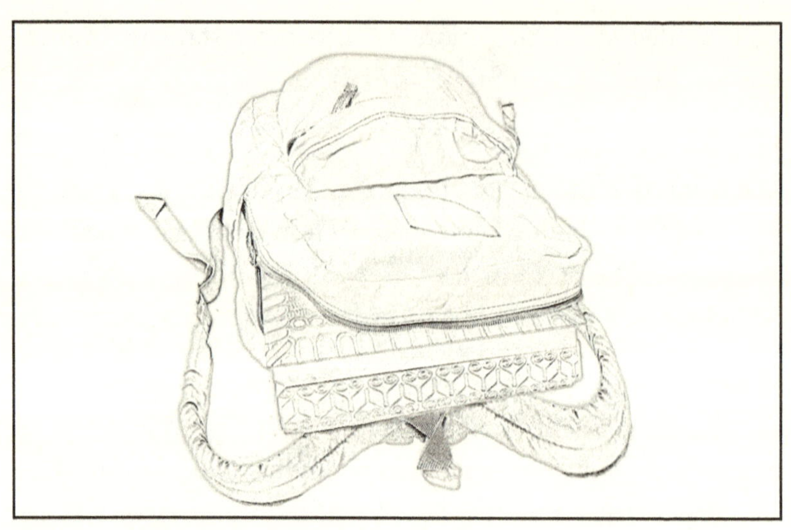

FINDING THE HIDDEN DRAWER
Chapter 15

John figured it was best to leave Cam as he was, asleep, clothed, and on top of the bed. John turned off the lights in their room. He used his phone's flashlight to look over the box he had gotten that day. He turned his back to Cam's bed to keep the light from waking Cam. Though, thinking about it, he knew he'd have to shoot off a cannon to wake up Cam. Cam's light snoring confirmed John's thoughts about Cam being sound asleep.

All the same, John tried to be quiet. He sat down on his bed and put his backpack on the floor. John unzipped the bag at the top of the pack and reached in for the box. It had more weight to it than he thought it would. The box had designs on the outside of it that were made of wood carvings which had been attached onto the lid and sides. It all looked to be painted a silver color and had a few dings and scratches on it.

At first, he had bought the box as a present for Ruth. She seemed to like it and it went well with the gift of the necklace. Since what happened at the museum, he didn't know if it was safe for her. Now, he was taking his time opening the box. John wasn't so sure of his ghost hunting skills lately. He had seen that Katie was the real ghost hunter among their group. Ruth was no doubt the second most gung-ho ghost hunter. He had rated Cam as the least, but now he was thinking it had turned out to be himself. John took 10 minutes before he could pick up the box and put it on his lap. A game of "should I or shouldn't I" ran through his head. Finally, he figured he should.

He ran his fingers along the top of the box and saw where the hinges were in the back. He slowly lifted the lid, his heart pounding. He thought something bad would be in the box. Afraid that it might jump out at him, he stopped. Then, he thought since he had come this far, he had to go for it and lifted the lid.

A wave of relief came over him when he saw that the box was empty. He realized he hadn't been breathing until then when he exhaled a sigh of relief.

A layer of red felt lined the box. There weren't even any dents in the felt. *Looks like it had been empty for a long time. Yeah, I guess Ruth wanted this box to keep her jewelry in or something*, he thought.

When he tilted the box to return it to his backpack, he felt something slide inside it. It was only a little shift. He almost didn't feel it. Now, as he shifted the box back and forth, he was sure there was more inside the box. Again, he slid his fingers along the edges and found one piece that moved when he pushed it. But nothing else happened. A more careful look showed that there were two design pieces that would move. When he moved both at the same time, a small hidden drawer slid open a few inches.

John looked up. He thought he saw Cam moving, but it wasn't Cam. He wasn't sure what it had been, but nothing looked like it did, or could move. His mood quickly changed. He started getting nervous. The strange smell had returned. He knew he needed to focus on the drawer. He wanted to get that done and put it away for the night.

He pulled the drawer open a little more and saw a stack of strange looking papers inside. They were tied with some old, yellowed string. When he picked them up, a low buzzing sound started in his ears. He found it hard to take his eyes off the newly found papers. Black squiggly lines filled the pages. His second look told him it was a language he did not know. He knew he couldn't read it. *Maybe it's old English writing, seeing as we are in England,* he thought. All he was sure about was that he didn't have a clue what it said. He couldn't make out any letters or words at all.

He thought to relook at all this in the morning when he would be thinking more clearly. He put the papers back in the secret drawer. Then, he closed it up and went to put the box in the backpack. "Ouch," he called, catching himself before he got too loud. Somehow, he managed to cut his finger on the box. *Must have a sharp edge somewhere,* he thought, and used his thumb to stop the bleeding. He grabbed a tissue from the nightstand and wrapped it around his finger. After that, he finished putting the box back in his backpack.

John now turned his thoughts to getting ready for bed. The bed was calling. In spite of starting to rehash the events of the day in his mind, he was asleep right away. That night the dreams returned.

- 77 -

ROOMMATES ONCE AGAIN
Chapter 16

Getting into a comfy bed at Ruth's house thrilled Katie. But to be honest, getting any rest was thrilling. She joked with herself that even the floor was looking good to her. Though, unlike Cam, she did get ready for bed before jumping in. "Oh, and I brought my jimjams," she joked. Ruth laughed. It was an inside joke made during their time at school in Romania.

The last thing Katie recalled before falling asleep was Ruth saying, "Don't worry about not seeing any ghosts. We signed you up for a ghost tour of Stratford tomorrow night."

A shower and clean clothes put Katie into a good mood the next morning. Getting to the breakfast table gave her a new drive. Going on a ghost tour of Stratford made her feel even better.

"You look chipper," Ruth said, as Katie came into the kitchen.

"I feel chipper," Katie said. "Hey, what did you say about a ghost tour as I was falling asleep?"

"Right," Ruth said. "John and I booked a ghost tour for the four of us tonight. I knew you wanted to do some ghost hunting while you're here. I've never been on the tour, but I have heard it's a proper ghost tour," Ruth said. "Of course, it should be good. I live in a very old and haunted town. But there are no ghosts in my house." Ruth said that with a sad look on her face. "Newer build, I suspect."

"That's fine," Katie laughed. "At least this way I'll get some sleep. So what will we be seeing tonight?"

"We'll be going to a few 'haunted' pubs and taverns. Also, we'll go to the hotel that Shakespeare's daughter, Susanna, died in. Oh, and we'll also go to a plague house."

"A plague house?" Katie asked.

"Well, there's no plague there now," Ruth said. "At least there shouldn't be, I think."

As was often the case, Katie didn't know if Ruth was joking. Katie knew the plague once killed massive numbers of people in England and Europe. The victims of the plague often had blood and pus seeping out of large, swollen sores on their necks. They suffered with lots of pain before dying. She also knew it has been under control for many, many years.

"Thanks, Ruth. I'm looking forward to the tour. I'm just so glad to be here with you and the boys," Katie said.

"I'm quite over the moon that you all are here, too. So, after you've eaten, we'll pop over to see the boys. We can stop and do some shopping on the way, if you'd like."

"That'd be great," Katie said.

In the kitchen, Ruth made some soft-boiled eggs and toast for her and Katie. Katie filled the water kettle on the counter and turned it on. Then, Katie got two cups hanging on hooks under the upper cupboard along with matching saucers. Lastly, Ruth finished making the tea. It wasn't long before the two sat down at a table with egg cups, toast in a wire rack, butter, jelly, and steaming cups of tea. Katie felt it was all so quaint there in England. It was like some of the old novels she loved to read.

JOHN AND CAM
Chapter 17

John woke when he heard Cam getting ready for the day. John hadn't slept well. He only just fell back asleep after being awake half the night, so he was tired now. "Cam, I've got to tell you something," John said. He hoped he was awake enough to know what he was saying.

"Hey, John, it's great to be here and Ruth looks great. Still as quirky as ever. I'll bet you're happy to see her," Cam said.

"Oh, I'm happy to be here and to see Ruth, but there are a few other things going on." John sat up in his bed. "That box I bought for her yesterday at that strange antique shop from that old woman..."

"Yeah," Cam replied. "I meant to ask what she said to you as we left there."

"I'm not sure, something about the past. It didn't make any sense to me. Some crazy things have happened with that box. First off, when I had it in my backpack at the National Gallery, it disappeared for the security guy. He looked in the pack and it was empty. I took the bag, and I could feel it was in there. I watched him, but he never took it out. So that was weird thing number one," John said as he held up one finger.

"Then, later, Ruth couldn't see the box in the pack, but I could. Weird thing number two." John held up two fingers.

"Let's see. Number three was last night, here in the room. You zonked out fast, but I took a better look at the box. I found a secret drawer in it. Inside it's got crazy old papers. I can't even read the writing at all. I'm not sure what language it's in."

Cam's eyebrows arched, his eyes opened wide, and the edges of his lips curved down while he listened to what John said. He was trying to take it all in when John continued his count.

"Last, number four, my dream last night was scary, scarier than I've had in a long time. In the dream there was this kid. He had to be dead. He was so pale. He had huge black sores on his neck and face. In the dream, I went over to Ruth's and knocked on her door. The door opens and the kid just stands there for a second before he jumps out at me. He almost got to my throat before I stepped back. Then I fell backwards down the couple of stairs by her door. I never did hit the ground though. I just kept falling until I woke up."

"Are you making this up?" Cam asked John. Cam's eyes had narrowed, and his lips formed a puckered shape.

"I wish," John said. "I don't know, Cam. I used to be so much better with this ghost stuff. For some reason, I'm having a tough time with the possibility of it."

"I'm right there with you. I've never been good at handling the idea of ghosts. You know that ghost from my grandpa's ship scared me to death. I mean, sure, I'm a lot better about it now. Maybe it was Katie and how well she handled her ghosts in

Transylvania that helped me a little more. And hey, you were the one who led me to Katie and helped me with my ghost."

"I'm thinking I'll need to call in Katie and Ruth to help out if this box comes with that creepy kid in my dreams," John said.

The sound of John's parents moving in the other room gave him pause. John added, "And let's not tell my parents about this until we have to."

Cam gave John a knowing nod.

The two boys started getting dressed for the day. John called out, "Mom, Dad. We're almost ready, so we'll go ahead and get breakfast downstairs."

John's parents didn't respond. "Do you think they heard me?" he asked Cam.

Again, the boys could hear someone moving around in Jill and Tom's room. Suddenly, there was a loud crashing sound, like something big fell over in the parents' room. The two boys' heads snapped around to look at each other. They couldn't imagine what had happened in John's parents' room to make such a huge noise. Also puzzling was that his parents weren't saying a thing. No 'oops,' swearing, or 'we're okay.'

"Are you okay?" John shouted out. "Mom, Dad, are you okay?"

When there was no response, both boys jumped up. John got to his parents' door first. He knocked and said again, "Mom, Dad, are you okay?" His voice filled with concern. He hated to invade their privacy by just going in, but he knew something was wrong. He pushed open the door, "Mom, Dad?" and stuck his head inside the room.

Cam wasn't sure what was going on. John left the door half-way open and then stood there. "What is it?"

John pushed the door open the rest of the way. As the door opened, the boys could see into the room. The sheets on the bed were pulled up, but otherwise, nothing was out of order in the room. There wasn't a thing there that looked like it could have made such a loud bang as they had heard.

The two boys stood there, looking into the parents' room, dumbfounded. "How could that be?" Cam asked. "There aren't any other doors to this room, and we both heard all that noise."

At that moment, the main door to the suite opened. Tom Sadler walked in and said, "Hey boys, glad to see you're up. Mom and I went down for breakfast, but I forgot my glasses. I came back up for them."

The two boys shared a look between each other and then back into the parents' room. Neither one knew quite what to say.

Tom, seeing the boys by his bedroom door, asked, "What are you boys up to?"

John said, "We thought we heard you and Mom still in your room. When we talked to you, no one replied. We thought we'd better check it out."

"Oh, okay." Tom walked into his room and picked up the glasses off his night stand. He put them in his pocket and turned to the boys as he walked to the main door. "Don't wait too long to come down for breakfast." And with that, he went to rejoin Jill downstairs.

John turned toward where he had left his backpack with the box inside. He could only stare at it.

Cam's shoulders quivered and a cold feeling came over him.

John's stare broke when he caught the smell of that odor that he had been smelling lately. "Let's not tell my parents about this, either."

- 85 -

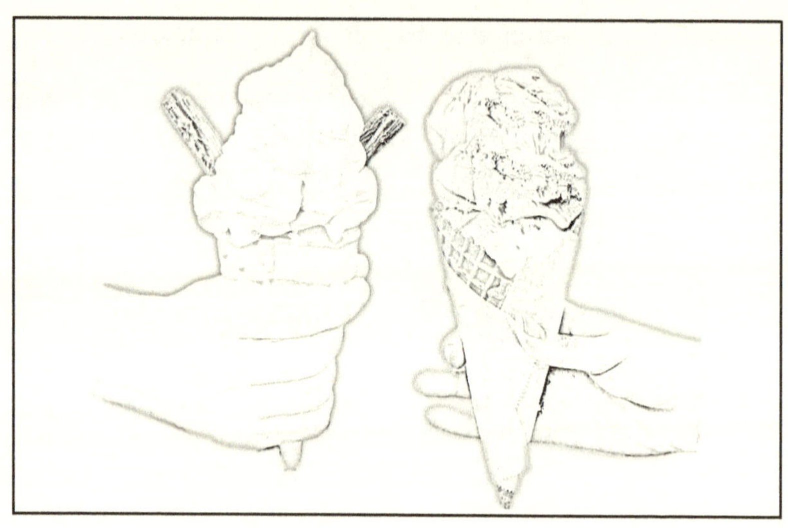

GHOSTS AND ICE CREAM
Chapter 18

The boys ate little for breakfast for two reasons. Their morning 'meeting' was the first reason. Meeting up with the girls in an hour or two for lunch was the second reason. John had thought to tell the girls about the box before. Now he also had to tell them about what happened in his parents' room, too. He knew there was no way to explain the room. But he hoped Ruth and Katie might have an idea about the box and its papers. He figured there might be a library or something like that where they could ask about them.

After breakfast, walking around in the sunlight helped John and Cam feel a lot better. The boys had texted the girls. They would meet near Shakespeare's house since Cam and Katie had not seen any of Stratford yet. The boys knew it would be a crazy day.

Walking to the house, the teens all found themselves meeting on the street about a block away. It wasn't surprising since both roads funneled to the street where they agreed to meet.

After pointing out Shakespeare's house to Cam and Katie, John said, "Okay. I've got to tell you something." As he said that he saw an ice cream shop across the street with some outside seating. "But first, would you like some ice cream? We can sit over there."

"Not for me," Katie said, "too early."

Ruth agreed with Katie.

"Too early for ice cream?" Cam asked. "That can't be a thing."

"You guys get your ice cream. We can sit outside while you tell us what you need to tell us," Katie said.

So the boys went in and got some ice cream cones. The girls sat down at the small outdoor table. The size of the ice cream cones the boys came out with surprised the girls. "What you're going to say must be big. That looks like enough ice cream to talk here for hours," Ruth joked.

"Well, yeah, maybe," John said. Cam could only nod because ice cream filled his mouth.

The boys sat down, and Cam turned to John in a show of giving John his full attention. Cam was hoping that John would explain it all.

John started to feel a little nervous. He felt he put himself on the spot, but he had to say what he wanted to say. "Ah, well, you know that shop we went into yesterday morning in London. The old antique shop?"

The others nodded.

"Well, I bought something there that I didn't tell you about," John said.

"You don't need to tell us each little thing you buy, John. Why would you think you should?" Katie asked.

"It's going to affect you, or at least it might," John said. "What I bought was the box that Ruth was looking at, that silver colored box."

Ruth was a little confused. She wondered, *did you buy it for you, or was it supposed to be a present for me since I found it?* John answered Ruth's unasked question before she could ask it.

"At first, I bought it for you, Ruth. I saw that you liked it and I thought it would go with the necklace I got you." John blushed a little when he said that. "That weird old woman at the shop put it into my backpack. I didn't even touch it until last night."

"Oh, how sweet of you. I do hope you are going to give it to me," Ruth said.

"Ah, well, I'm not," John said.

"Oh, I guess you weren't being as sweet as I thought." Ruth said. Again, she gave a confused look.

"Really, Ruth, that's a good thing," John said. Now Katie also looked confused.

"The box might come with a ghost, so you don't want this box, do you?" John said.

"Well, perhaps not," Ruth said.

"You'd better explain a bit more," Cam said.

"Yeah, I guess you're right. When I looked at the box last night, I found a secret drawer in it. Inside the drawer it had some papers. They looked super old, but I don't know how old they are. I can't even read the writing that's on them. I don't think anyone can read it. It might be English, but I'm not sure," John said.

"So, you think it's haunted because you can't read the writing?" Ruth asked.

"No, I think it's haunted because it seems to have vanished and then showed up again.

"Well, that does sound like it might be haunted. Where'd you leave it, back at the hotel?" Katie asked.

A sheepish look came to John's face. "I've got it right here in my pack," John said.

"Oh, and don't leave out the part about the ghost stuff that went on in your parents' room this morning," Cam added.

The girls did a quick double take at Cam. "We need to get some ice cream, too," Ruth said.

WHY YES, I DO HAVE A HAUNTED BOX

Chapter 19

They all talked over what took place in the Sadler's room but thought it best to focus on the box. They discussed it long enough to go and grab some lunch as well. They were able to find a table at a food stall that was still open.

John pulled the box out of his backpack to show the others. This time the box didn't vanish. He was happy about that. Katie said it might be because it's daylight out now. At least, that was the only reason they could come up with.

John was able to open the drawer and pulled out the papers. "John, you'd better leave those in the drawer. We need to find out how old those might be first," Katie said.

"Good catch," Cam said. "The oils from your hands could damage the papers if they're super old."

Before he put the papers away, John thought to take some photos of them with his phone. *I wonder if haunted notes would show up in a photo?* It was a happy surprise for him that the photos he took came out.

The teens thought it would be best to ask around to see where the papers could be looked over. "John's plan to take it to a library sounded good," Ruth offered.

"You can show them the couple of the pages on your phone," Katie said. "We don't want something to happen to the papers."

Everyone got on their phones and searched for the best place to ask about the papers. At first, they didn't know where to start other than searching for someone who could translate the pages. But they had no luck with the websites they found.

Katie asked Ruth, "Do you have any friends that might know something about this kind of stuff?"

"Well, there is one friend who's sister is at uni," Ruth said. She gave her friend a call while the others waited to hear what Ruth was saying. Sadly, her friend couldn't get with her sister right away. Ruth would have to wait until later when the friend's sister was free.

The rest of the day, the teens just hung out. They shared what they knew of their friends from summer school and what they were up to.

Night Time Ghost Tours
of
Stratford-Upon-Avon

🐾 Each Wednesday night
🐾 From 19:00 to 20:30
🐾 Group sizes 5 to 13 people

**Meet at the Swan Fountain
in Bancraft Gardens**

GHOST TOUR AT NIGHT
Chapter 20

John's parents met up with Ruth's father, Kwame, for dinner. Their plan was to go to some pubs that Kwame told them about, where locals played music. They planned to eat a little something at each of the many pubs and listen to their local music. "So, you couldn't convince John and the others to join us tonight?" Kwame asked the Sadlers. "It's local English music."

The Sadlers knew that the pubs were okay, even for their kids to be in, but they knew the teens preferred their ghost hunting. "No, there was no way the local music could compete with a ghost tour by night," Jill Sadler explained.

"I suppose so," Kwame replied, shaking his head.

The teens went to a fast food grill to get their fill of burgers and fries. After eating, they headed to the swan fountain in the park where the daytime city tour met.

"The tour does sound like something I know you and Katie will like," Ruth said to John.

John was glad Ruth was looking out for him, but he wasn't sure if he wanted more ghosts. *I'm not sure about the one I'm dealing with now,* he thought. He was glad he wasn't alone.

"Good evening, all," a man dressed in black said to the people waiting by the fountain. A second man joined the first. They were both wearing short, flat black hats and black capes that hung to their knees. The men had gray hair, and the first one had a beard.

"Welcome to our tour. Please, we must insist that you all stay close by. Some of the footpaths may be wet or icy. Also, some spots will be dark, so please mind your footing. We don't want to lose one of you again."

The word "again" brought some nervous laughs from an older couple on the tour. "Keep this in mind. You are on this tour at your own risk." Then, the man with the beard pointed across the river. "Let us begin."

The group started the short trek down the path to the Royal Shakespeare Theatre. It sat just a short walk away from the swan fountain. The tour guides told of several ghost sightings inside the playhouse. Most of the sightings were of ghosts backstage while a play was going on. Actors and stage crews have reported seeing ‹ghostly spirits› in costumes from plays not performed at that time.

"Have you ever seen a Shakespeare play," Ruth asked her friends, "other than the one we went to, John?"

John was happy to see that he had one up on Cam and Katie. Neither of them had ever seen a Shakespeare play. Of course, he had a hard time getting any of it.

"I guess they have them back home, but we've never seen one," Katie said. Ruth was a little surprised at their response.

John noticed Ruth's surprise. "But he was from here, where you live," John pointed out.

"Yes, that's true. You'll have to see one the next time you can," Ruth said.

Cam had seen little pieces of Shakespeare's writings around the town. It made him think he wouldn't be able to follow a play if he did see it. To him, the shirts John got his parents were about as much Shakespeare as he would ever get into.

As the group left the theater, John was a little surprised. He thought the guides would have tried to scare them. He wondered if they'd do something later on the tour.

PLAGUE AT

THE TUDOR WORLD MUSEUM

Chapter 21

After leaving the playhouse, the group walked along Sheep Street. "We're on our way to one of the oldest taverns here in town. It dates back to the 1250s. It's called the Shrieve's House. It's said to be the most haunted pub in town," the guide said. He led the group down a short alley to its entrance. Once there, a woman met them. She carried an old lantern.

The teens couldn't help but see the sign that said, NO CHILDREN ON NIGHT TOURS. Katie and Ruth were getting worked up, hoping to see a ghost. Both John and Cam were getting a little worked up too. They were hoping *not* to see a ghost. But both boys knew there was no way they could just wait outside, so they followed the girls inside.

At first it took John a minute to get used to the dim light of the lanterns in the rooms. The tavern was now a museum so there were lots of old, creepy displays all around the rooms. Because of the old age of the building, the floors were uneven. The ceilings were very low in most places. Cam chose to keep a hand on Katie's shoulder. He wanted to stick closer to her and not bump into things. John saw that and did the same with Ruth.

"The Shrieve's House has a long past," the guide said. "It's been many things through the years: a home, a tavern, and a school room. Several deaths have taken place here, too. People claim to have seen as many as 40 ghosts. The most often seen ghost is that of a little girl. Back in the 1700s, townsfolk tortured the daughter of a maid here because they thought her mother was a witch. To get the mother to confess, people first burned the little girl's hands, and then her feet. Lastly, they sliced open her belly."

John could feel Ruth's shoulders shudder when she heard that. Ruth turned around to John and said, "How could they be so cruel?"

John could only shake his head. He couldn't make any sense of it either. The story added a heavy feeling in the room. The shadows seemed to be getting longer and darker. That awful smell was there again. John wondered, *Is this something the museum did to amp up the horror of the times they were showing? Or worse, should he expect his ghost?*

"Keep an eye open. People have seen a little girl playing in some of the rooms here at night. Sometimes her guts hang out." Katie knew they told the story to add to the spooky feeling. Still, she couldn't help but think that so much evil could have had some lasting effect.

It was very soft, but John thought he could hear the sound of a laugh. He stopped and tilted his head to see if he could hear it better, but he didn't hear it again. "Did you hear that laugh just now, Ruth?" he asked.

Ruth raised an eyebrow as she turned and looked at John. "No. No, I didn't hear any laughter, and I hope I won't."

A quick ripple of jitters ran through John's shoulders and arms. *Keep holding onto Ruth*, he thought. And then a laugh came again. John was the only one who twisted his head to look around. He kept walking.

The group came up to the next display and stopped for a moment. The guide shone the lantern near it. It was a bed with a dummy lying down in it to show a sick person. Standing over the bed was a dummy cloaked in black robes and wearing an odd looking mask. The mask looked like a strange bird with a very, very long beak-like nose. That was how doctors dressed during the plague. They put herbs in the long nose. They hoped the leaves would filter the air they breathed and keep them safe. *I wish I had one of those masks. That way I wouldn't have to be smelling that now*, John thought.

The guide swung the lantern to the side to light up one more part of the display. It lit up a figure of a boy who stood next to the doctor. The boy was staring at John. Seeing the boy startled John and he jerked back a bit. He hadn't seen a boy there before. Then, just as fast, the guide swung the lantern back to that part of the display. The boy was gone. John couldn't be certain that it wasn't only a creepy part of the display. But the more he looked, the less likely it seemed. He was almost certain that it was the boy he'd seen near Shakespeare's house on the tour.

"Ruth, did you see that boy?" John asked, still looking where the boy had been standing.

"A boy? No." Ruth said. "Don't you recall? Children are not allowed on this tour."

"Did you see something?" the guide asked.

"Um, not sure," John said. "Looked like a boy, but only for a second."

The startled look on the guide's face turned to one of concern. "Let's move along," he said.

UP CLOSE AND PERSONAL
Chapter 22

John kept his hand on Ruth's shoulder as they walked out of the plague room. The smell seemed to stay with them. Ruth followed the last guide into the next room while John turned to look back. To do that he had to take his hand off Ruth's shoulder. He shouldn't have done that. As soon as the light left the room, in the shadows, the boy walked towards John. He stopped within inches of John's face. The boy's face was ashen and dripping sweat. There were strange bumps on the boy's neck. John couldn't help but let out a cry of surprise. The only thing that stopped him from running out of the room was that Ruth and the guide were blocking his way out.

The guide in front of Ruth stopped and turned his head towards John looking to see what was going on. John put his hands on Ruth's shoulders and started to direct her along past the guide. John felt a little safer when he and Ruth passed the guide and was able to be within the light from the guide's lantern. When John risked a look back, there was only the guide standing there scratching his head - no strange boy. John turned back to Ruth and the others.

"I just saw the kid from my dream and from Shakespeare's house," he quickly said to Ruth.

"If he is here, we'd better keep closer to Cam and Katie," Ruth said.

You don't have to tell me that, John thought. At this point he passed Ruth and took her hand. For a brief moment, his thoughts moved from being worried to how nice it felt to hold Ruth's hand. Ruth gave John's hand a squeeze. He would gladly have stayed there holding her hand until he felt a cold chill. The chill reminded him where he was. With a squeeze of Ruth's hand, he led Ruth towards Cam and Katie. He only felt better when they reached the other two. John kept hold of Ruth's hand.

"What just happened, John?" Katie asked. "Did you see something we're not seeing?"

"I did," John said. "I keep seeing a boy. First in a dream after I got here in Stratford. Other times I've seen him in windows and walking behind me. I don't know if he's following me, or if I keep running into him."

The tour group moved along. John made sure to stay within the lantern light.

"Keep an eye out for the ghost of a girl named Alice," one of the guides said. "She died here of the plague in 1564. Her ghost can be seen here playing in the nursery. We'll be coming to that spot soon."

"Do you think it might have been the little girl you saw," Ruth asked John.

"No, I'm sure it was a boy," John said. Just then, a book flew towards John and hit him on the back of the head. It pushed his head forward, but it didn't do much else other than scare him more than he already was. The book had opened while it was flying so it wasn't too solid when it hit him.

"Ouch," John said, as he rubbed the back of his head.

"Are you alright?" the guide asked as he rushed up to John. "That might have been Alice. I'd heard of her ghost throwing things before, but hadn't seen it myself, until now."

"Yeah. Yeah, I'm okay," John said, still rubbing the back of his head. "I think I'm going to quit the tour here. I'll meet you all outside by the entrance."

"I'll lead you out," one of the guides said. He was used to having people so scared that they left the tour early. He held up his lantern to light the way.

Ruth kept her hold on John's hand. "I'll go with you," she said.

As the two followed the guide downstairs, a loud bang went off by one of the doors they passed. It sounded like someone had pounded on the door as hard as they could. The teens and the guide jumped.

"You really shouldn't have effects like this to scare people on the tour," Ruth told the guide.

"I, I, don't know what that was," the guide stuttered. He looked quite shaken. "We don't have effects like that." Unseen by John and Ruth, the look on the guide's face started to match the scared look on John's face.

The loud banging came again. To John it sounded like someone had kicked the door. He didn't want to wait to see if it would open. John and Ruth turned towards the guide. It surprised them to see he had started out of the room. They hurried along to catch up to him. They couldn't help but notice the guide had picked up his pace in leaving the building. John and Ruth matched his pace. No one looked back, nor said a thing until they went out the front door.

"Blimey," the guide said. The three quickly walked the length of the courtyard to get to the street. They were struck by the contrast between what they had just experienced and what they were now seeing. The streets were brightly lit with lots of people doing normal things like shopping at the market booths.

John had a lot to think about. On the one hand, he was still shaken up over seeing what he knew was a ghost. Even worse was getting a book thrown at him by one. He didn't believe that it was the ghost of Alice. He felt it was most likely the ghost of the boy who had been stalking him. But he did feel better because Ruth was standing next to him. She was leaning into him and had her arms around his.

"Wow, and there's still more places to see tonight on this tour," John said. He wasn't sure what to think about that.

VISITING THE PLAGUE HOUSE
Chapter 23

After the rest of the tour group came out of the Tudor Museum, everyone was talking. They all wanted to know if John was hurt. They also wanted to see if that was something staged or if he had met a real ghost.

Like the guides, John reassured them that it hadn't been staged on his part. "Nothing that I was in on," he said.

"Looks like you've found a poltergeist," Katie said to John.

"Or maybe more the other way around," Cam joked.

"Thanks," John said, making a face. *I'd rather not either way*, he thought.

His friends were glad to see John wasn't hurt or too badly shaken. John did take the chance to keep Ruth's arms around his while they walked farther along High Street.

A few minutes later, the whole group stopped behind the two guides. The guides had been filling the walk so far with stories about the famous author of Stratford. "Across the street, on the corner, is where Shakespeare lived at the time of his death. Sadly, nothing is left of the house today. It's a garden now.

Sitting as long as it did after his death, the house was not fit to live in. The new owner had it torn down before long. It wasn't until a few hundred years ago that the city bought the land. They made this park to honor the land's former owner."

"High above us are these three level Tudor style buildings. Today, they are known as the Garrick Inn and the Harvard House. The buildings are thought by some to be the starting point for the plague. They boarded Plague victims inside these buildings so they wouldn't spread the disease. Mostly, one's loved ones brought food and meds to them, but they couldn't leave. In fact, it is believed Shakespeare's own son, Hamnet, who was only 11 years old, was locked in this building. Like so many others, he would die there. His body was buried in the Holy Trinity Church graveyard," a guide said.

The guide had just finished saying that when John found himself being swung around by his backpack. It seemed to be twisting him around. He found himself not only facing the street but wobbling towards it. *Who pushed me?* he thought.

John spun around so fast that his arm had slipped out of Ruth's grasp. John was lucky that Cam was standing near him. Cam reached out and grabbed John's pack. Both Cam and John ended up swirling around. They stopped just before either one stumbled into the street. The guide in the mustache also reached out to stop the two boys before they could go into the busy street.

"Steady on lads," the guide said. "What happened?"

"I saw John, out of the corner of my eye, spin around and start falling towards the street," Cam said.

"It felt like someone grabbed my pack and spun me around," John told them. He knew it must have been the ghost, but he knew no one would believe him if he said that.

"I didn't see anyone behind you, son," the guide said. "You just became this spinning top."

John was getting mad about what the ghost was doing to him. "So, nobody grabbed my pack?" John asked.

A woman in the group said, "No, I had just been looking your way. It looked as though something hooked onto your pack and spun you around. You're lucky. Your friend and the guide stopped you from ending up in the street."

"You've had a bit of a night, haven't you?" the guide said.

"It sure seems so," Katie added. She envied John for his ghostly visits since she hadn't seen any ghosts on this trip. But, she couldn't say she missed any danger that came with the visits.

"Let's move across the street," the main guide said to the group. "You'll be able to get a better picture of the buildings from there." They all followed in crossing the street at the corner. Once there, the guide pointed out the open space at the corner behind them. "This spot was once the site of a bake shop. It belonged to good friends of William and Anne. They were such good friends that they named their twin children after the couple. You might know their names, Hamnet and Judith Sadler.

Although the guide kept talking, Katie and Cam couldn't help but stare at John. Katie said to John, "Did you know about this? Why didn't you tell us?"

"John, you mean you didn't tell them about your royal status?" Ruth asked. Ruth couldn't keep the smile from coming to her face as she said that.

John could only look down and shake his head. "Ok, so sue me. With all that has been happening since you got here, I forgot to tell you guys. Sorry." Talk of the Sadlers distracted John from thinking about the ghost that was bothering him. Ruth could see the look on John's face lighten with the change in topics.

"Royalty?" Cam asked.

"Nooo," John said. "You would have had to have been there. The daytime tour guide said we Sadlers are like Stratford royals because of our name. We don't even know if we're family to those Sadlers."

"No, but John's father said he was going to look into it with a genealogist here in Stratford," Ruth said.

"So, are we supposed to bow when we see you or wait until they say it's true?" Cam teased.

"Do you think you are one of 'The' Sadlers?" Katie asked John.

"Well, that would be cool," John said, "but I don't think so. Dang, maybe. I don't know." John would like to think it's true, but he never heard of any family in England before.

They all stopped talking after the tour guide made a loud effort of clearing his throat.

John took one last glance at the building across the street. There was a flash of light in one of the windows. Then it darted to a second window pane, and a third after that. The flashing appeared in almost all the window panes jumping around with no pattern. The lights had caught the eyes of all those in the tour, along with the two tour guides.

"Blimey," the mustached guide said. "To our good fortune, our next stop is for a bit of rest from the tour, just here. I'm sure we could all use a good cuppa." He led the group two doors down High Street to where it turned into Chapel Street.

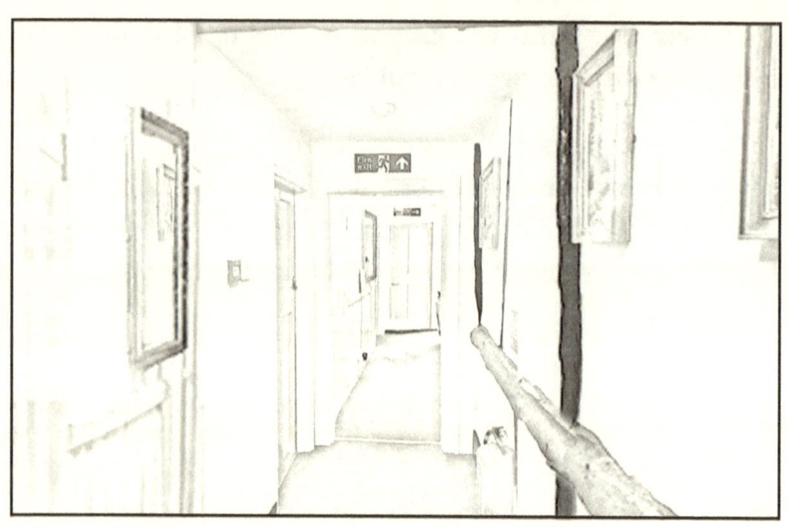

THE SHAKESPEARE HOTEL
Chapter 24

The group paused in front of the old Shakespeare Hotel on High Street. The building looked like so many of the timber framed buildings in Stratford. It was a white building striped with dark vertical boards.

"Welcome to the Shakespeare Hotel," the guide said as he led the group inside. "This grand hotel was once the private home of the Bard's daughter, Susanna. She and her husband, John Hall owned it. Among the several ghosts said to haunt this hotel is Susanna, herself."

"You are in for a treat tonight. We'll have a look upstairs, and we'll be having a cuppa and a cake for each of you."

"A cuppa?" asked Cam.

"Yes, a cup of tea," Ruth said.

"Oh, it'll be nice to get something hot to drink," Katie said.

"And something to eat," John added.

"Yes, John," Katie said. "...and something to eat." She shook her head at how John was always ready to eat.

"We'll go up to Susanna and John Hall's bedroom first to see where she died," the bearded guide said.

The bearded guide waved to the young girl behind the hotel's Front Desk as the group filed past. She nodded in response since the tour came there often. The guide led them through a large comfy looking room with a fireplace. From that room they went up a set of stairs and down a hallway. Near the end of the hallway was a door with a sign, 'Susanna & John Hall.' "We'll just be able to look in from the doorway. This is the room in which Susanna Hall died, there in that bed with the cover above it. We're told that the cleaning staff has seen her ghost lying in that bed."

"After you've looked, please find us downstairs. We'll meet by the fireplace where we came in. The hotel has tea and cakes for us as part of the tour. See you there." After that, the guides started downstairs. The guests mostly just took a peek into the room and then followed the guide back down the hall.

Just the four friends stayed standing by the bedroom door. "Wow, that's a bit creepy," Cam said.

Katie looked in for a second, and then she and Cam started for the stairs. Katie called back, "John, Ruth, are you coming?"

"Give me a minute," John said. "I'll be down. I just need to see something."

"What's going on, John?" Ruth asked. "I thought you were hungry. And, after all that's been going on with you tonight, I thought you'd like a break. Or, is it that you'd like some alone time with me?" Ruth half joked.

"Both are great reasons, but since I've gotten into this hotel, the box in my backpack has been moving on its own. I just need a minute to think what to do next. It's moving a lot gentler now than it was down the street." John just looked down at the floor. John's whole body language showed he was nervous. He wanted to do something, but didn't know what. He had run out of ideas.

Ruth could see John looked a little defeated. "Since the others have gone downstairs, I'm going to try something I saw before on the tour. Promise me you'll be strong." With that, Ruth reached in and flipped off the room's light switch.

Ruth's actions surprised John at first. His eyes took only a second to adjust. By the sliver of light going into the room, he saw a figure lying in the bed! His eyes became huge, his head lurched back, and his mouth dropped open. John started to take a step back, but stopped when he saw it wasn't the ghost of the boy. Also, he didn't sense that foul smell the ghost boy seemed to have. Ruth almost glowed from the results of her test.

"You can do this, John," Ruth said as she nodded.

"Hello?" John said into the room. He forced himself to stay there and not move back.

"John Sadler. Come closer, closer, closer," the figure said. Her words echoed throughout the room.

With big eyes, John turned his head to Ruth. The look on his face asked, _should_ I _do this?_ His voice said, "How does she know my name?"

"Go on," Ruth said with a blink of her eyes and another nod of her head.

John was able to find some courage from Ruth and walked farther into the room. He stepped over the rope that blocked access into the room. The ghost turned her head towards him. "You have something of mine," she said.

John had a guess but wasn't sure just what she meant. "I do?" He hoped it was only the old box that the ghost was talking about. He didn't want to have to give up the papers.

"You have my story," she said. "You have my story".

"Your story?" he said. Again, the box in his backpack moved and grew cold. Shivers ran up and down his arms. He didn't think he would be able to walk any closer to the figure. He wasn't sure if he needed to give it back to the ghost, or if he could keep it. He was also a bit afraid of what the ghost might do to him for having her story.

"Come here, John Sadler," the figure said again. "In your bag."

There was a kindness in the woman's face that was missing from the boy's. It made him feel safer. John knew he would have to give the papers to the ghost. He swung the backpack to hang from one strap with the bag in front of him. He pulled the top open and lifted the box part way out of the bag. "Do you mean this?" he asked.

The figure nodded her head. She moved slowly and looked as if she were very old and in poor health. She pointed to the box.

"I wrote that story. Elizabeth, my daughter, kept it in that box. I so wanted my father to know about it. I wanted all to know about it."

John and Ruth didn't know what to say. John could only hold up the box with his shaky hands.

"You've read my story, haven't you?" the ghost said.

"No, no, I haven't read it." John said it louder and quicker than he had wanted to. He was nervous. He didn't want to make the ghost mad at him for reading it. "I looked at some of it, but I can't read any of it. Is it in English?" John asked.

"Yes, of course it is, but not the English you speak now. It's the English of my time."

"Then, I need to ask you more about the papers." But, before John could say any more, flash! The lights of the room flashed on. The bright light made them both shut their eyes and turn away from its source. They turned to see who turned on the lights. A young girl with cleaning supplies stood in the doorway. Her eyes were huge. She seemed almost frozen in place. "You … you … can't be in here," she managed to say, never taking her eyes from the bed.

John and Ruth both swiveled their heads to the bed, but all they saw was a neatly made bed. There were no signs that a person was ever in the bed.

"What was that?" the girl asked, not able to move. She kept staring at the empty bed.

Neither John, nor Ruth, wanted to stick around and get in trouble. Since the girl wasn't speaking, John pushed the drawer shut and slipped the box back into the bag. The two stepped back over the rope and rushed down the hallway. It surprised them that the girl didn't follow them, but they weren't going to ask her why. They knew why. The voice of the girl repeating, "What was that?!" grew faint as they ran down the hall. Loud thuds pounded on the doors of each of the rooms they passed. Holding hands, John and Ruth picked up their pace until they got to the bottom of the stairs.

Cam and Katie just finished their tea. The whole group was getting up at the urging of the guides. Katie and Cam had surprised looks for Ruth and John. "You were gone so long. What were you doing?" Katie mouthed.

"Gotta tell you later," John said as he reached for some pastries with a shaky hand. "You won't believe it."

"John? Food, now?" Ruth asked.

"Hey, it's part of the tour," John said with his mouth full of his first bite. "And, it'll help me feel better," he was able to get out. He was careful not to spit out any crumbs as he spoke to Ruth.

ON THE WAY TO THE HOLY TRINITY CHURCH
Chapter 25

The tour went on to the Holy Trinity Church. The guide with the mustache led the group while the other guide was at the end of the group. Each one answered the questions of the guests while adding their own ghost stories.

The four walked side-by-side, arms joined. John and Ruth walked in the middle. "Okay, what's the story?" Katie asked. "You both looked spooked."

"We were!" John said. He told Katie and Cam what had happened at the hotel and at the plague house. While John gave them the basics, Ruth filled in as much of the details as she could recall. After they finished their stories, Katie said, "We've got to get someone to tell us what that story is about."

"I know, but who?" John questioned.

"I'll have to give that a think," Ruth said, and she tapped the side of her head.

"Any guess who the ghost boy is?" Cam asked.

"Other than trying to kill me, he hasn't really said much," John said.

"Why do you think he'd want to kill you? I'm guessing it must have some link to the box and the story," Katie said.

"I don't know, but I wish I did," John said. "I'd like to get him to stop before he succeeds."

"Well, that would be nice," Ruth joked.

"You think it might have belonged to him when he was alive?" Katie asked.

"Well, there is at least one person who owned it, perhaps two," Ruth said. "The ghost himself, and the ghost of the woman from the hotel, too."

"True," John said. "I know who I'd rather ask, the woman. She hasn't tried to kill me yet."

"You do make a good point there," Ruth said.

"We can talk more about it after the tour ends. We have this last stop at the Holy Trinity Church and then it's done," Cam said.

"Please keep up with us," the guide in the front of the group called back. "We do hate to lose guests," he joked, "and we are coming up to the graveyard."

TRINITY GRAVEYARD – LAST STOP
Chapter 26

In the dark, the graveyard looked much spookier to John and Ruth. It didn't look as scary when the Sadlers and Enams went there together. Katie and Cam had not seen it yet, so they had mixed feelings. Walking along the path with ancient graves on both sides thrilled Katie. She wondered about the lives of those who had died so long before. Cam, on the other hand, only saw the weather worn headstones. Many headstones had names carved into them that were no longer deep enough to read. Many leaned to the side and looked like they might fall over at any time. Cam hoped that this wouldn't be that time.

As the group neared the halfway point of the path, John felt like he walked into a dark closet. He could see the graveyard and the church in the distance. Only now no one from the tour was to be seen. He couldn't see Ruth, Katie, or Cam. He spun around. It looked like they had all vanished. His heart started to race. He spun around a few more times, hoping to see someone, at least one soul. On his third spin he stopped sharply. There, in front of him, about five feet off the path and into the graveyard stood a small boy. The boy was dressed in old clothes and didn't look well. This boy didn't have sores on his neck and face. But he did look like the boy John had run into before.

"You?!" John said. "You're the one I've been seeing. Who are you? Why are you stalking me?" John second guessed himself after he said this, thinking maybe he should feel threatened by the ghost. *Did I really just stand up to a ghost?*

"You have my story, story, story. Give it back! You can't read it." The ghost's words echoed in John's ears. The ghost reached out towards John but stopped short. He didn't seem to be able to come closer to John than he already was.

Since the ghost wasn't coming after him, John felt a little safer. Safe enough to not run. Besides, he didn't think he could get his feet to move. His legs felt as though they were glued to the ground. John said, "What do you mean, your story? I bought this. Well, I bought the box, and it came with it. And who are you?"

"Hamnet, and you must not read that story. No one can!" the boy said. "You'd better give it back right now or you'll be sorry." While he spoke, the boy seemed to get an evil thought. He started laughing about it in a way that caused more chills to run along John's arms and shoulders.

John slid his backpack off his shoulder and onto his one arm. He wanted it in front of him, and his arms were around it. He felt a hand grab his shoulder. As he spun around, he came face to face with Ruth. "John, come along." she said. "We need to stay with the others."

As John glanced up he saw the tour group about 10 feet ahead of him still going into the church. Now, it all looked just as it had before the boy appeared. The nearby houses and buildings were all lit up for Christmas. People were walking around in the park. Both Katie and Cam stood with the rest of the group, except they were looking back at John.

"What did you see this time? Or should I ask, who did you see?" Ruth asked. "You've been standing here staring at that grave."

John's glance spun around again between Ruth, the grave, and the tour group almost at the church doors. "I was talking with Hamnet. At least that's what he said his name was."

"Hamnet? Wait, do you mean that Hamnet?" Ruth asked as she pointed back to the grave.

John's mind kind of stopped as he was trying to process what he was seeing and hearing. There, among the graves where he had been staring, was a small sign. It said, 'In memory of Hamnet Shakespeare 1585-1596 buried in this churchyard.'

Again, more chills came over John, and he felt very cold. He put the backpack back over his shoulders and took Ruth's hand. They hurried to the group. As they walked, John said, "This is crazy. I think it might be that kid. I'm not sure, but that's a great place to start looking into this box I've got."

TALKING IN CHURCH
Chapter 27

The tour guides brought the group up to the front door of the Holy Trinity church. The guide with the beard pointed out that the church is open during the day for people to go inside. "There, by the back altar, you will find the grave of William and the sign placed there. It warns people to not disturb his bones. If they do, his ghost will curse them. Also buried there are his wife, Anne Hathaway, daughter Susanna, and son-in-law Dr. John Hall. We're not allowed to conduct our ghost tour inside the church, so this is where we will end tonight's tour. Of course, feel free to go into the church on your own. There is an extra fee to go to the back altar where Shakespeare and most of his family are buried. Or you can look around the main part of the church without an extra fee. We hope you all enjoyed the tour. We enjoyed sharing our Stratford-Upon-Avon with you."

The four friends gathered at the back row of the pews. John and Ruth sat down while Katie and Cam stood. "I had a chance to look around the other day," John said. "I'm going to sit here and think some things over. You three can take your time and I'll wait for you here."

"I can show you and Cam around," Ruth said to Katie. "I've been here many times." So, Ruth started showing her two friends around the church. They walked up to the first altar and peered towards the front of the church. There was a sign across the walkway. It said that part of the church wasn't open at that time. "We can come back later since you'll be spending more time here in Stratford."

"Yeah, that'd be fine," Cam said.

The three teens spent five more minutes walking around. After that, they found their way back to where John was sitting.

When they got to John, John didn't seem to notice them. "Hey, John, you still awake?" Katie asked.

John shook his head in surprise to hear his friend next to him. "Oh, sure. I was thinking." John stood up and swung his backpack over his shoulder. "Cam and I can walk you back to Ruth's house."

"That'd be nice," Ruth said. "We can get some hot chocolate if you like."

"Sounds like a good way to end the evening," Katie said.

John looked a little sheepish. "Well, I don't think that'll be the end of it," he said. "I need to talk to you about what's happened tonight."

They all followed John, curious to hear what he was going to say. Before he said anything though, he led his friends out of the church. They headed for the path to the street instead of taking the shortcut through the graveyard. From the street, they walked along the path between the park and the river. On the way, John explained what had happened. He told them about his latest encounter in the graveyard.

When the four got to Ruth's house, Ruth's dad asked how their 'haunted tour' went. "Just as we thought it would. Chased by headless ghosts, had to dodge swinging swords, that sort of thing," Ruth said. Then she laughed and looked to see how her dad took her joke. She didn't want to tell him what really happened. She knew he would worry about her.

"Just like when I was a kid," he joked back.

At first, Cam wasn't 100% sure Ruth's dad was joking. He didn't know how many ghostly things Ruth and her dad might have seen before. After all, this was England. Many of the ghost stories he had read as a kid took place in England.

John knew that Ruth's dad was joking. Still, he didn't want to share his recent meetings with ghosts with her dad either. He wanted to impress Ruth's dad by being a 'normal' boyfriend. As soon as the word 'boyfriend' came into John's head, he had to stop and think. *I guess that's what I am, Ruth's boyfriend. Or at least, that's what I want to be. Hopefully, she wants me to be, too.*

"We're going to make some hot chocolate. Would you want any, Dad?" Ruth said.

"Thanks, but I've got to get ready for bed. One of us around here works for a living." He gave Ruth a kiss on her forehead. "Don't stay up too late."

"Good night" was said almost at the same time by all of the teens. Ruth headed off to the kitchen to make the hot chocolate.

YOU JERK!
Chapter 28

The friends went to sit down in the room Ruth called their 'snug.' They all had cups of hot chocolate topped with plenty of whipped cream floating on top of the steamy drinks.

There were two chairs and a small couch in the small room. It was quite warm and cozy due to the fire burning in the fireplace. John took a sip of his drink. Then he said, "Well, let me tell you what I saw and see what you all think."

He began to tell the others about the ghost woman at the hotel and what she had said. Then he told them about the ghost boy at the old pub. The last thing he told them about was running into the boy in the graveyard.

The others sat very still while they listened to all John was telling them. Without knowing it, as John talked they all started to move inwards. They wrapped their arms around themselves and brought their legs up. It wasn't long before they were kind of in the shape of balls. It was John who noticed it when he was ending his stories. He couldn't help seeing their intense body language and the look on their faces. So, he did what he thought best to lighten the mood. Loudly, he said, "Boo!" and jerked towards them. When everyone jumped back, John said, "Gotcha!"

"You jerk," Cam joked. Then he gave out a little nervous laugh followed by a soft punch to John's shoulder.

"Sorry, I deserved that, but you all looked so intense that I had to."

"You quite deserved that," Ruth said. To be playful, she hit him with the small pillow she had been holding in front of herself.

Getting back to the subject, Katie said, "It sounds like you've made a friend of Shakespeare's son, Hamnet. Though I wonder what his link to the box and papers you found is."

"And what are those papers?" Ruth added. "We're going to need someone who can tell us what they are. Everyone agreed. "Most likely, we can work with the few photos you took after you first found the papers."

"That should work," John said. "Ruth, if you could do that since you live around here that would be great. I think you must have a better idea than I do on where to start."

"Yes, that'd be fine. I'd love to help."

"I'll send you the pictures I took so you'll have those."

"Brilliant," Ruth said.

"We'd better get going," John said as he stood up. He gave Ruth a hug while Cam gave Katie a quick kiss.

The two boys turned out of the gate and started walking into the night. The street felt different than when they had come to Ruth's house. John felt it. He could see Cam did too by the way Cam kept looking back over his shoulder.

After a few minutes, John looked over to Cam. He said, "We need to make one quick stop on the way back to our hotel."

Cam didn't like that idea, but he wasn't going to go on by himself. He had an idea of where John wanted to go, but didn't ask. It was where he would want to go himself - back to the ghost woman.

IS SHE STILL THERE?
Chapter 29

The ghost woman's hotel was only a few blocks away. *We've got to take the chance*, John thought. He and Cam headed there. His biggest worry was that they might not be able to get back to her room. It was late and he was no longer on the tour, but he knew it would be worth an ask.

Christmas events in the old part of town meant that the hotel had a larger number of guests than normal. Guests were coming and going much more than on off-season days. John and Cam walked into the lobby and went straight to the front desk. They asked the young girl working there if the Susanna Hall room was still open to peek into. At first, she told them it was too late. Paying guests were staying on that floor and couldn't be disturbed. Cam said, "Are you sure we couldn't just go for a peek into the room? I'm leaving Stratford in the morning and didn't get a chance to look at that room. It's part of my school paper I have to write when I get back home. My English teacher will give me extra credit. I didn't get a chance to come here before." Cam hated to lie to the girl, but he knew they wouldn't bother any guests. Plus, he wasn't sure if the ghost would make herself appear during the day. After a minute of the two boys looking rather sorry, the young girl gave in to their request.

"Alright, but be quick about it, and don't make any noise. I'll be checking up after you in five minutes," she said.

The boys didn't waste any time getting back to the room. The door was still open, and the rope was across the doorway like before. Cam stayed in the doorway while John stepped over the rope and went to the bed. When he nodded, Cam turned off the light switch as they had arranged.

There on the bed sat the ghost of the old woman.

"Uh, uh, I'm back," John said. He wasn't sure what to say to a ghost. He knew he didn't have much time so he amped up his courage and started talking. "You know my name. How did you know my name, and who are you?" John asked.

"You are John Sadler, Sadler, Sadler," her voice echoed again. "You are family of my father's closest friend, Hamnet Sadler." Chills ran along John's arms.

"Hamnet?" John asked. "So, my ancestor was Hamnet Sadler? That's the ghost I keep seeing, Hamnet."

"That boy, that boy is . . ." Her words cut off mid-sentence when the lights flashed on.

John looked to the light switch, but there was no one there. Cam was on the other side of the doorway looking down the hallway. When Cam did turn his head to look into the room, his face had a surprised look. "How'd the lights go back on?" Cam asked.

"Did you do that?" John asked. "Quick, turn them back off."

But, before Cam could reach over to the light switch, he heard the desk clerk coming down the hall. "Your time is up!" she said.

What!? That wasn't five-minutes."

"Hurry up, before she sees you," Cam said.

John hopped over the rope to stand between the rope and Cam as fast as he could. By the time the clerk got to the doorway, she couldn't tell that John had gone over the rope.

"Sorry, but my boss asked what you were doing. He said it was too late for non-guests to be up here. You'll have to come back." She wasn't thinking about what Cam had told her before about leaving Stratford.

"Okay," Cam said as he tugged on John's shirt to exit the doorway. The boys started walking down the hallway to the stairs followed by the desk clerk. Half way down the hall John seemed to walk into a wall of that foul smell. As they walked through it, pounding started on each door and came towards them. All three started running in fright the rest of the way and down the stairs.

At the bottom of the stairs, the clerk asked, "What was that?"

TO SLEEP OR NOT TO SLEEP – IS THAT THE QUESTION?

Chapter 30

The boys left the clerk standing at the bottom of the stairs. They didn't stop to answer her question. A second later, they were out into the street.

"So, do we know who the ghost was that pounded on the doors?" Cam asked.

"I think it must have been that boy's ghost that keeps haunting me. I'm still not sure who he is, at least, not 100%."

"Don't you think he's the ghost of your ancestor? Didn't the ghost of the woman say he was your ancestor?" Cam asked.

"No, she didn't get a chance to say who the boy is. I don't know. There's a lot in play on all this," John said. "It's been a long day and night."

Cam was feeling confused. "Let's drop it for now. I'm too tired to follow what you're telling me."

"It seems like the ghosts are trying to confuse us," John agreed.

"Let's just get back to the hotel and get some sleep," Cam said.

The two boys didn't say much after that as they walked the short block to their hotel. John's dad was sound asleep when the boys came in. John's mom had gone to bed, but managed to say, "Did you enjoy the tour?"

"Yeah, it was cool," John said.

"Great, we'll talk about it in the morning," Jill managed to say before nodding off.

On their nightstands, the boys each found a bright red package of candy. "Oh, good, the candy fairy has been here," John said. On closer look, the boys could see that they were Cadbury Chomp bars. It took them only moments to eat their candy bars.

The candy bar gave Cam a brief burst of fuel. He sat on his bed and asked John, "Ok, so what did the ghost tell you this time? I didn't hear her well."

John sat on the edge of his bed facing Cam. In a quiet voice, so he wouldn't wake his parents, he told Cam what the ghost said. He tried his best to repeat it just as he heard it. He hoped that it might make more sense this time.

"So, your boy ghost is named Hamnet, right?" Cam asked.

"I don't know. The old ghost just said I was a relative of Hamnet Sadler."

"Ok," Cam said, nodding his head.

"But, when I asked if the boy ghost is my relative, she only said 'the boy is…' That's when the light came on, and we lost her. So, I guess he might be my ancestor, but what if he's Shakespeare's son, Hamnet? Or, he could be some other Hamnet. If there are two Hamnets, there could be more."

"It's an odd name," John said. "But who knows?"

"Let me check online for any other Hamnets linked to Stratford." John picked up his phone and started searching. It only took a couple of seconds for his search to come back with some results. "It only shows two Hamnets linked to this town. I don't know if there were others that aren't showing up here, but there are two. Hamnet Sadler, the baker, and Hamnet Shakespeare. Are you finding any pictures of either of them?" John asked.

"Well, if I did, they're not there now. My phone just died. I don't get it. I was at 50% when I started looking. Now, it won't even turn on," John added.

"Crazy. Mine's dead too. Even plugging it in is doing nothing for it."

"OK, that's freaky," John said. "My head is almost spinning, I'm so tired. Either that candy bar wasn't enough to wake me up, or I'm crashing after a sugar high. I'm going to bed. I can plug my phone in to charge tonight."

"Sounds like a plan. I'll leave mine plugged in and see what I've got in the morning."

The two boys got ready for bed and turned off the lights. They were asleep in only a few seconds after their heads hit their pillows.

In John's dream that night he found himself drowning in a huge vat of dough. He kept sinking as it was being stirred. He reached out to a woman that was standing there. Sometimes the woman looked like Ruth and other times it didn't. While he was trying to keep his grip on her hand, the boy from the graveyard was pushing John's head down. John woke with a start, having trouble breathing and not able to see a thing.

FINDING PROFESSIONAL HELP
Chapter 31

It took John a second or two to grasp that he had his face buried in his pillow. He raised his head and looked around the room. He saw that the sun was just coming up. It was early. After he reached over and looked at his phone, he knew it was too early to be getting up. He turned over and was asleep again in moments.

John woke up for a second time. *Wait, my phone showed the time,* he thought. He opened his eyes to check on the phone again. It was 100% charged and working now. He could see that it was now close to 9:00 a.m., so he thought to get up. Cam was still sleeping but started to stir after John's bed squeaked as John stood.

A dazed Cam shook his head and checked his phone. "Good news. My phone is charged now."

"Old news, but I'm glad to hear it. I'm going to throw on some clothes and get something to eat downstairs. Are you coming?"

"Sure." But Cam closed his eyes and let his head flop back on the pillow.

John was going to say something, but just then his parents walked in. The sound of them saying, "Hey, aren't you up yet?" was enough to get Cam moving.

John and Cam ate breakfast with John's parents in the hotel's breakfast bar.

"So, what are you and the others up to today?" Jill Sadler asked John.

"Not much. We're going to hang out with Ruth and Katie," John said. "What do you and dad have planned for today?"

"Ruth's dad gave us the name of a genealogist here in town. He runs that genealogy shop we saw on the tour of the town. We're going to look up your father's blood line," Jill said.

"Very cool," Cam said.

"Funny you should mention that," John said. "We heard again on the ghost tour that the baker who used to be here in Shakespeare's time was named Sadler. Also, I have it from a good source that we might be related to him. That would be cool."

Tom Sadler thought John's 'good source' was someone on the tour, but he didn't go into it further. "Yes, it would be. I guess we could be, but Sadler sounds kind of German to me. Your grandpa never talked about where he was from," Tom Sadler said.

"No, Jim, you might be wrong. I'm pretty sure it's English," Jill said. "We'll find out today. And, if I'm right, you owe me a big, fancy dinner," Jill said. She gave her husband a grin.

"And what do I get if I'm right?" Tom asked her.

"You get a big, fancy dinner!" Jill said as her grin turned into a big smile.

"I see," Tom said. He knew he was better off not testing his wife's logic. Besides, he was going to take her out for a big, fancy dinner anyway, but she didn't know that. He smiled to himself.

After breakfast, John and Cam met up with Ruth and Katie. The girls waited on a bench in the main park along the river. Cam sat right down next to Katie. That left John just enough room to sit next to Ruth. To fit better, John hooked his backpack over the back edge of the bench and squeezed in next to Ruth. Ruth gave him a smile.

"It's kind of sad to see there are so few vendors left from the Christmas Market," John said.

"Yes, they're not here for long, but it's great while they are," Ruth said. John could see Ruth's smile fade. He thought she was sad about the market ending, but it was the thought of him leaving soon that saddened her.

He thought to take her mind off the market ending. "Have you found any place where we could take the papers? We need to see what they say on them," he said to Ruth. "I still can't make out any part of what they say. I don't know how people could ever read that writing back in the day."

"Yes, the uni at Birmingham isn't too far from here. I was able to get online with the librarian. She said we should get the papers checked out by someone in their school. Since the papers are old, they have people there who know all about old writings. They can figure out what is written and how old it might be."

"Sounds like just what we need. Did they say how to do that?" John asked.

"Yes, she gave me a phone number for the group that does that. They're used to looking at old things like that. Also, she told me about a local campus here in Stratford. It's only down the street from your hotel. It's called the Shakespeare Institute. We could drop by there and see if we can talk to someone right away. If nothing else, they could direct us better after seeing the papers. This is getting more and more thrilling," Ruth said.

"For sure," Katie added. "Oh, by the way, what happened last night?" Katie asked John. "I know you and Cam didn't go back to the hotel and straight to bed." She knew Cam and John well.

"Were you tracking our phones?" John asked.

"Of course. We've had that on our phones since summer school." She had a sheepish look on her face.

"I forgot, but no problem." John said. He was fine with her being able to track his phone. When they were going to school in Romania, that app came in handy.

"Yes, we did stop at the hotel again to talk to the ghost there."

"Was she there?" Ruth asked.

"Yes, we got to see her, but only for a minute or two. She said I was a descendant of the baker. She was about to tell us who the boy was before the lights came on again and she vanished."

"Yeah, we still don't know how the lights came on by themselves. Neither of us was near the switch when they did," Cam added.

"That was too bad," Katie said.

"It was bad, the lights I mean. I think the switch is old and maybe not working right, or maybe it was that boy ghost. I've been smelling something strange when he's around, and I smelled it last night as we left," John said.

"You mean as we were chased out of the hotel by some crazy loud banging on all the doors we passed?" Cam asked.

"You should have seen that desk clerk run," John said to Ruth and Katie.

"Yeah, the desk clerk," Cam said mostly to John. "Good thing we were able to outrun her so she wouldn't run us over."

The girls laughed. "Too bad she wasn't as used to ghosts as you are, John," Ruth joked.

John knew it was time to change the subject. "Let's check out the school," he said.

"I hope we'll have some good luck there," Katie said.

"I hope so," John said. He turned and reached to the back of the bench to pick up his backpack, but it was gone.

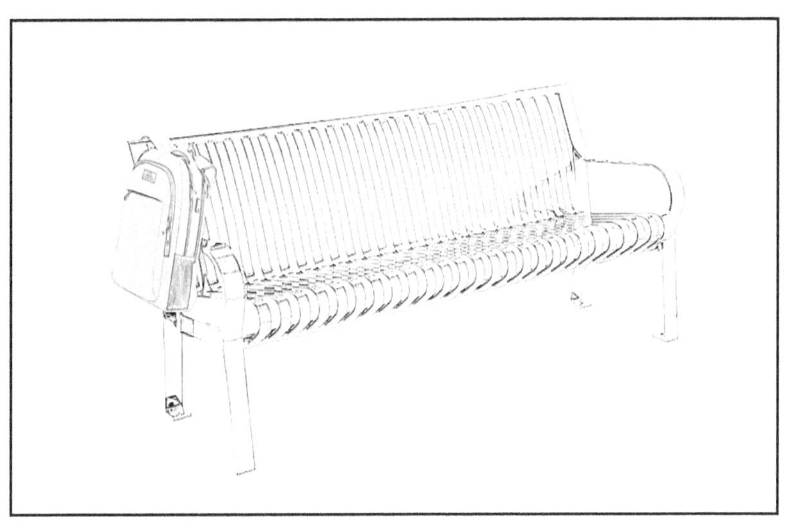

IT'S GONE. NOW WHAT?

Chapter 32

"What?!" John said. "My backpack is gone! It was right here."

"Oh, my gosh," Cam said.

"Cripes," Ruth said. "I was sitting next to you this whole time. I didn't see a soul near your bag. How could someone have nicked your bag?"

"No one came close to you that I could see," Katie said. She shook her head. "Of course, the box with the papers was in there, wasn't it?" A gloomy look came upon her face.

"Yep," John said. He looked up and down the street, but there was no one walking around. No one had his bag that he could see. John walked around the bench a few times, making a fist and punching into the air.

The others gave John a minute to get some of his anger out. Then, Ruth said, "We could let the police know." Then she gave it a bit more thought. "But it seems like half the people walking around town have a backpack on. Plus, there's all these extra people in town. I doubt that they would, or even could, do a thing."

"Just in case, Cam and I can walk up the street this way," Katie said. "You and Ruth go that way," she said to John.

The teens agreed and started out walking down the streets. Despite closely looking at all the backpacks that looked even remotely like John's, no one found the pack.

Ruth took John's hand in hers as they walked. John gave her a smile and kept walking. "I'm not holding out much hope that we'll find it," John said.

"I'm afraid I agree," Ruth said. "How could your bag just vanish like that."

"I have one thought," John said. "In a word- Hamnet." He mulled over walking to the graveyard but thought to leave that for later.

"Oh, my. He has been a nasty bugger, hasn't he?" Ruth said.

"I'll say. But I can think of a few options for now. I wonder if the hotel ghost can be of some help in getting the papers back. She seemed to be friendly, or at least she didn't try to throw me into traffic," John said.

"Yes, that's always a good sign."

"And, we still have some pictures of some of the pages. I'll bet that the people at the Institute can tell us what the papers were about from those pictures. Maybe if we knew that, it might help us find them again," John said.

"Brilliant," Ruth said, and she gave his hand a squeeze.

John returned the squeeze. Then he looked into Ruth's eyes and added, "Thank you, Ruth. I know I should be feeling bad right now. The box and papers are important. Losing them is a major problem, but being with you seems to make everything better.

"I feel the same way," Ruth said.

MEETING UP
Chapter 33

Cam and Katie were at the bench in the park when John and Ruth got there.

"No luck I see," Katie said.

"Only the bad kind," John said. Then he plopped himself down on the bench. "I did come up with some plans. Maybe the ghost might help. And I still have photos on my phone of the papers. Maybe the Institute people can tell us more about the papers from those. It might help us find them, if Hamnet took them."

The friends all agreed to John's plans. They'd have to wait until that night. It needed to get dark to be sure to see the ghost in the hotel. Luckily, the sun set at around 5 p.m.

"That'll give us time to eat dinner and then get over there." John always took meal times into consideration. "So, where do you want to eat lunch?" John asked.

"There's a truck with some good Indian food," Ruth said. "It tastes great and it's not far from here."

"Sounds good to me," Katie said.

"And we can keep an eye out for your backpack," Cam said. John nodded.

Within ten minutes, the friends arrived at the food truck. They had looked at each backpack, just to make sure it wasn't John's. Sadly, no one they saw had John's bag. They lost focus on their search when they neared the food truck. A heavy smell of curry filled the air around the truck. They all got in line to order. John's dad surprised them when he walked up behind them. "What's for lunch?" he asked.

Tom Sadler didn't get the response he thought he would. Everyone seemed very quiet. They barely said hello. Jill Sadler stepped up a second behind her husband.

"You're all looking rather glum," Jill said. "Is something wrong?" It hadn't taken Jill more than a quick glance to know something wasn't right.

"Oh, it's my backpack. Someone took it off the back of the bench we were sitting on at the park."

"Did you see who did it?" Tom asked.

"No. We all walked around looking for it, but no luck."

"That's lousy," John's dad said. "You didn't have your passport or phone in it, did you?"

"No, I just had some things that I bought today," John lied. He didn't want to tell his parents about the box and the papers yet.

"Oh, Johnny. You're going to love your mother, even more than you do all the time." Jill Sadler told her son. The smile on her face made John wonder what she had in mind.

MOM TO THE RESCUE
Chapter 34

"Did you forget how you had to carry my iPad in your pack when we came to England? How I didn't have room in my carry-on?"

"Yeah." John still wasn't sure what his mom was getting at, but the smile was still on her face.

"I must confess I wasn't sure you'd watch your pack. You leave it all around. So, I put one of those tracking tags in your bag with my iPad. When you gave me the iPad back, you didn't give me the tag. I bet you didn't know it was in there. We might be able to see where it is right now."

John's first thoughts were, *I don't leave my things all over! Well, on my last trip I did lose my phone, but I got it back. And my passport went missing for a little while too. Ok, maybe Mom is right, this time.*

Cam and Katie both voiced their relief. John relented and said, "Yes!" He closed his eyes and gave a slight fist pump. "Thank you, Mom."

Jill Sadler's face beamed with pleasure. She was glad she was able to make her son and his friends feel better. She thought not to stress the fact that she hadn't fully trusted her son not to lose his bag.

Jill opened her phone to look for the item, but it wasn't showing up. "Sometimes the tag doesn't show up. It needs other people's phones to be near it to pick up the signal. We need to give it a little time. Meanwhile, I can share the tracker with you, John. You'll be able to see where it is on your phone." He felt a great deal of relief. John's joy quickly faded because he couldn't see the place where the tracking tag was right away.

Cam saw the change in his face and knew what happened. "You might have to wait a little bit before you see where the tracker is. Like your mom said, it probably shouldn't take long."

"I hope that will help," John's mom said. "Your dad and I are going to see that genealogist, so we've got to get going. Let me know if you still can't see it in a little while. Love you," she said as she gave him a hug.

John's dad gave John a pat on his shoulder and nodding smile before he walked away with his wife. "We'll let you know if it takes longer than we expect."

John looked at his friends. "Ok, what do you want to do until you can see where the tracker is?" John asked.

TALKING TO PEOPLE

AT THE INSTITUTE

Chapter 35

"We're quite close to the Institute. After we eat something, let's stop there before finding the thief?" Ruth asked. John nodded yes.

The food took a little longer to get than planned. To save time, they all ate as they walked.

Soon, they found themselves in front of a two-story, red brick building with lots of white framed windows. To the left of the door was a plaque that said, 'The Shakespeare Institute, Birmingham University' on it. Ruth opened the heavy-looking wooden door. Ruth led the way as the others followed her inside to the lobby.

A young girl sitting behind the lobby window greeted them. John started telling the girl about the old papers they had found. He wondered if anyone there could look at the photos he had of the item. John didn't tell them right away that he no longer had the papers with him. He worried they might tell them to find someone else to ask.

Katie thought the girl was very patient with these strangers who had such an odd request. The girl picked up her phone and called someone who must have been in the building. "Dr. Robins will be with you straight away," she said. "Please take a seat until then."

They only had to wait five minutes before a young woman came down the stairs. The woman had short blond hair and a friendly smile. After greeting them, she asked the four friends to follow her down the hall. The group came to a large room with lots of windows, both in the walls and the ceiling. The windows looked out to a garden. Inside the room there were several comfy looking chairs. Dr. Robins asked them to sit down. "So, Sarah said you've got some old papers you've found. May we look at them?"

"Well, for now, I only have pictures of about the first 6 pages on my phone," John said. He felt a little ashamed for not being able to produce the real papers.

"For a quick look now, that would be fine," Dr. Robins said. John pulled up the photos on his phone and handed it to Dr. Robins. She looked at the first photo and then zoomed in to get a better look. She slid between a few photos, zooming in on each one. As she did, her eyes got bigger, and she got closer to the screen.

"Where did you say you found these papers?" she asked.

John told her how he found them in the drawer of an old box he bought in London. That started a lot of questions. "What did the box look like? What size are these pages? Were there any other things in the box?"

John tried his best to answer all her questions. Though, he did have two questions of his own. "Can you read that writing? Are there any dates on it?"

"Well, yes! I can read it. There is a date at the start of it. It appears to be dated 1619. Oh, my!" Dr. Robins said. The teens could tell that she must have seen something that caught her eye.

"Wow, that's crazy old," Cam said.

"Cripes, that is old!" Ruth said.

There was a new mood in the room. "Are you sure?" Katie asked.

"Oh, quite sure. Now, if it was indeed written then, and by the name on the first page…. But we'd have to see the papers and make some tests," Dr. Robins said.

"Whose name is on the first page?" Katie asked.

"The name is Susanna Hall." Dr. Robins said.

"Shakespeare's daughter?!" Ruth asked.

"Yes, that Susanna Hall. At least, at this time, that's what this photo is showing. Whether it is real or not is yet to be seen. We will need an in-depth look at those papers," Dr. Robins said.

"But you say you found this?" Dr. Robins asked. She looked up at John and then the others with a doubting look. "Really?"

"Yes, in an old antique shop in London," Cam said.

As Dr. Robins further explained the papers, the teens got more and more amazed, as did the doctor. The time flew by. John's mind started to lose focus on what was being said. His mind took on a new focus. His focus was now on finding the stolen backpack. He knew he had to get those papers back, no matter where they were now.

FIND THAT BACKPACK
Chapter 36

John exchanged contact info with Dr. Robins. Then, John sent her a copy of his photos so she could take her time looking them over. They all agreed to meet back at the Institute the next morning.

Leaving the building, the friends were all talking at once, except John. He was checking his phone to see if the tracking chip showed where it was. "Yes!" He was in luck. It did. "It's at the graveyard," John said to Ruth. But, after giving it some thought, it almost seemed like a no-brainer that it would be there.

"I guess we're off to the graveyard then," Ruth said.

"You bet," John said. He immediately started walking.

"Wait a minute," Katie said. "Don't forget that kid ghost is a threat. If he's got your bag, John, don't expect him to play nice."

"I don't want to play with him at all," John said. "I just want to get the papers back. We'll see what happens when we get there."

They quickly walked towards the tall church steeple that stood above all they could see in the distance. Even though the evening sky was getting darker, the church was still an easy landmark to see. Before long, they were at the start of the path leading through the graveyard. John pulled out his phone to see where the chip was. He knew that the closer one got to the chip, the more detailed its place would be shown.

They all followed John as he led the way down the path. "It looks like the chip is down farther, near the church, on the left," he said. He pointed ahead, and they all started walking again. John looked back down to his phone each ten feet or so and the chip still showed the same place.

"I don't see someone there," Katie said.

"Me neither," Cam added.

"I'm just hoping we'll see the backpack. Maybe they left it there," John said. "It's still showing right over there, but I don't see it."

"I hope they haven't thrown the chip there and nipped off with the bag," Ruth added.

Their spirits all drooped at the thought that they could just be tracking the chip. The chip might not be with the bag or box.

They all followed John as he stepped over to where the signal showed the chip. As he looked up from the phone, he stopped.

"Oh, my," Ruth said.

John showed signs of defeat. *Why didn't I think to look here before?* he asked himself. There, attached to a pole in the ground was the sign he and Ruth had seen before. The sign read, 'In memory of Hamnet Shakespeare 1585 - 1596 buried in this churchyard.'

Cam knelt down right away to feel around through the grass beneath the sign. Katie and Ruth joined him in searching. There was no sign of the backpack being there. They hoped to at least find the chip. The ground was hard with no signs of having been newly dug up. "Nothin'," Cam said. He looked puzzled. "But the tracker said it was here, right?"

John looked down at his phone again and couldn't believe his eyes. "Now it shows it's inside the church, past the doors. It isn't moving, it's just sitting there."

"The game is afoot," Cam said. "I've always wanted to say that. I'm a big Sherlock Holmes fan and we *are* in England."

"Yes, Cam," Katie said. "Glad you got that out of your system." Then she started back to the path leading to the church.

"Hey, what better place to say that than here?" he asked. He got up and hurried off with the others.

HANGING AROUND
Chapter 37

The friends saw that there were only a couple of people in the front pews near the altar. They thought to spread out and look around the pews back by the door they came in through. No one could see the backpack. John viewed the map on his phone for what seemed like the millionth time.

"I don't get it," he said. "Now, it says it's right here, in the center of the aisle, just in front of the first pews. It's not moving, but I don't see it there."

They stood there looking down at the floor. No one could see the chip there. To anyone there it might have looked as though they were praying. That's what the priest thought when he walked out a door at the side of the church. John saw the door open and noticed something before it closed. There were stairs behind that door.

John signaled the others to join him in a pew near the door. When they were all seated, John leaned over to talk to them in a hushed tone.

"I think I know where it is," he said. "I mean, right now. Who knows? It could be gone by the time I get there, but I may be right."

"I didn't see it, but if you think you know where it is. Wait, where is it?" Ruth asked.

John looked back to the floor in the aisle where they had looked before. Now he raised his head to look at the ceiling. The others looked up too. "I don't see where it could be," Cam said.

"There are stairs on the other side of the door the priest just came through. I saw them before the door closed. I know there's a steeple on top of this church. It must have a doorway at the top of those stairs," John said.

"Wait a minute, John," Katie said. "This is a church and there are people in here. We can't just all march up the stairs. The door has a sign that says, 'No Entry.' The priest is right over there."

"You're right," John said. "That's why I have to go alone."

Cam and Katie were about to object when John said, "I can do this, but I'll need your help. I need you to distract all these people."

"Go on the other side of the church. Then, knock something down, or trip, or something, I'll sneak in there when they all look at you."

It only took a few seconds before Ruth said, "It should be simple. But, please be careful, John."

With that, she got up and walked to the other side of the church. Katie and Cam followed. Cam knew John would have a better chance alone of not being seen. He also figured John would only have to walk up there and back down. It should be easy.

John watched his friends move over to the other side of the church. He sat there praying that his bag would be there and that they wouldn't get caught.

When he heard the crash, he didn't even look over to see what happened. He saw the priest turn and start walking toward the noise. It surprised John at how easy it was for him to open the door enough for him to slip inside. He gently closed the door behind him, making sure it didn't make any noise upon closing.

The stairway was dark. He didn't dare look for a light switch in case the light might be seen from inside the church. He used the brief bit of light before the door closed to see where he needed to go.

The old wooden stairs wrapped around the inside of the tall stairway. He thought about the horror movies he'd seen. Someone sneaking upstairs always stepped on a squeaky step. He walked close to the sides. When he got to the top, he felt around. The door was at the top of the stairs, and he pushed it open. He looked over the lock from the outside to make sure the door wouldn't lock him out. He had to make sure he could get back inside later. He felt lucky that there was no lock on the door. *I guess no one sneaks into the church from way up here,* he thought. *No one in their right mind.*

A very strong, cold wind blew. John just wanted to get the bag and get out of there. He was freezing. He looked across the roof at the base of the steeple. There, he saw his backpack set in the notches of stones that made up the short wall. A strong, rotting smell blew into John's face.

When John reached for the pack, he felt a push from behind. It all happened in slow motion. First, he caught a glimpse of the stones by his feet, stumbling. He thought he should have known it, but he didn't. He had been caught fully off guard. He saw the stones of the short wall as he flew over them towards the open night sky. He didn't reach out fast enough. His first arm grabbed only air. His second arm to go over the wall did manage to grasp one shoulder strap of his pack. It was the only thing he could see to grab. He only knew his good luck when he felt the jerk of his arm. The pack's other strap caught on the stones. He wildly reached with his other arm. The only thing he could grab with his free hand was the strap he was holding. A split second later, his feet scrambled to find a place to grip. He didn't know what he was going to do.

There was nothing for his feet to catch onto. His feet kept slipping off what little hold he could get. The building didn't offer any place for his hand to hold on to either.

The strap of his backpack was the only thing keeping him safe. When he looked up, he saw the strap of his bag, caught on the bricks. Just beyond the pack stood the ghost of the young boy.

"Hey, help me!" John yelled out. "Please! Help me."

The boy stood there laughing at John. The pleasure in the ghost's face sent new worries through John. The ghost did just what John was afraid he'd do. The ghost reached towards the strap that held the backpack in place.

WHY'D YOU DO THAT?

Chapter 38

John's weight pulled the strap so tightly against the stone that no one could have loosened it. This seemed like the only good thing going for John at that point.

"You should not have brought that story here to Stratford. No one will ever read my sister's story," the ghost said, his voice an echo in the wind.

"What are you doing? Are you trying to kill me over a story? I know who you are," John yelled. "I know who you are."

The ghost stopped laughing. "How could you?" he said. A look of hatred spread across the ghost's pale face.

"You're Shakespeare's son, Hamnet. Your sister is Susanna. We were told what she wrote. The papers, we took them to someone who told us what they said," John shouted. John hoped that lying about knowing what the papers said might make Hamnet give up on killing him. His only hope was to make Hamnet think they had read all the papers. Maybe Hamnet just didn't want anyone to know what his sister wrote.

The ghost paused for a few moments but then started trying to release the strap with greater effort.

John hoped he could hang on long enough for help to get there. Downstairs, his friends were getting worried.

"I do wish John would hurry and get back here," Ruth said.

"Me too," Katie said. "It seems he could have gotten the bag and been back by now."

"Yeah. I shouldn't have let him go alone," Cam said.

"I'm going to go up there," Ruth said. "That had to have been that nasty ghost that tried to hurt John before who stole the papers."

"Probably," Katie said. They all got up and walked closer to the door. When the priest had turned his back on them, they tried the door to the stairs, but it was locked.

"It won't open," Cam said. A slight bit of panic started setting into Cam. *We've gotta get up there*, he thought.

"Can I help you children?" a soft-spoken voice asked.

Ruth, Katie, and Cam turned to find themselves looking right at the priest. The troubled look on his face did not match his kind voice. Katie quickly said, "Our friend wanted to try to get a view from the steeple. He went inside there and hasn't come back out yet." The words flowed out of her. She hated lying to a priest. She just knew she couldn't tell him about a ghost with a backpack.

The priest tried to open the door, but it wouldn't budge. "That's odd. It shouldn't be locked. Let me try the key." He reached inside his robe to his pocket. He brought out a key ring. But, when he looked at the keys, a confused look came across his face. "Strange, that key isn't here. I'll have to get the spare key." Then, the priest asked an altar server to get his key.

The friends' level of concern was shooting up. Their hearts were racing. They had wanted to run up the stairs, and now the priest was calmly walking to talk to someone. There was nothing they could do but watch things work in what seemed like slow motion.

Katie and the others were getting more worried with each passing second. "After hearing what Dr. Robins said about the story and who might have written it, I'm sure that it was Hamnet's ghost who took the pack."

"I agree," Cam said.

"It's time we get Susanna over here to talk to her brother," Katie said. "I'm not sure what else we can do."

"Katie, what if you and Cam dash over to the hotel where you've seen Susanna. It's not far at all. I'll stay here and hope the priest will get the door open. Plead with her. Maybe she can come here. She's got to."

"Good plan," Cam said. "Let's go." With that, the two ran out of the church. They only hoped John was okay.

TALKING HIS WAY OUT OF IT
Chapter 39

John's plan to distract the ghost seemed to be working. At least Hamnet was still talking and stopped touching the strap.

"You're lying, lying, lying. No one has read that story. They never will. They all left me there to die. I was just a little boy! Then Susanna wanted to tell people how wretched I was," Hamnet said. His words echoed each time he spoke.

"Those men with their beastly faces locked me up. Those long beaks. Taking my blood. They didn't let me out. That's my story!" Hamnet said.

"You had the plague," John said. "That was the only way they knew how to treat it back then."

"I was sick, but no one came. My parents and my sisters never came. They locked me away to die with all those others who were sick."

"There was no cure for the plague," John said. "Those men with the long beaks, they were doctors. They tried to help you."

"No, they locked me away to die. My sister ... she wanted to be like my father and write about how I died. She wanted to show the world how easy it was to lock me up, to forget about me."

"No, you're wrong," John said. He grew more and more worried. His hands were getting tired. Even with the night being so cold, he was sweating.

"We were always so close, but she never came to see me. They locked me in that place."

"What did she tell you?" John asked. He wanted to keep Hamnet talking. The cold was making it harder for John to hold the strap. He hoped Hamnet wouldn't notice him regrip the strap as his hands slipped. Maybe if this ghost talks long enough, the others can get here to help, John hoped.

AT THE HOTEL WITH SUSANNA

Chapter 40

Cam and Katie stopped outside the hotel entrance to catch their breath and to look inside. They hoped the desk clerk wouldn't be watching the door, but she was. As they had talked about on the run to the hotel, Katie would go inside first and distract the clerk.

Once inside, Katie was able to get the clerk to look away from the door. When she did, Cam ran inside and up the stairs. He had to talk to the ghost. It was their only hope to help John. He put his discomfort of being around ghosts aside. Although he didn't know what was happening with John and his ghost, Cam knew it couldn't be good. Cam stepped inside the doorway to Susanna's room and reached for the light switch. He flipped off the switch. In the darkness, Cam could see Susanna there at her usual spot on the bed. He didn't take the time to go in farther. He jumped right in talking to her. "You've got to talk to your brother!" Cam said.

"No, no, no!" Susanna echoed. "That is not possible."

"You've got to! My friend, John, is in trouble. Your brother took your story. We know you wrote about your brother," he said.

"Leave my brother alone. His life was one of tragedy. Let my brother rest in peace,"

"We'd love to leave him in peace, but his ghost is trying to hurt my friend. He is not at peace. I can feel it. I bet you can too."

Susanna's ghost sat silently for a moment with her eyes closed. "Why do you say that?"

"Because he tried to throw my friend into the street. Not only is he my friend, but his family was your family's friend. You know that too, don't you?" Cam said. He wasn't sure that Hamnet's ghost was trying to kill John, but he couldn't just wait to find out for sure.

"He's at the Holy Trinity Church right now with John and your story. They're on the roof. You've got to keep him from doing something really bad," Cam said.

The ghost sat there, not moving. Cam thought he wasn't getting through to the ghost. Cam's drive was replaced by worry. He didn't know what else to say or do when a bright light flashed. The lights had come back on in the room. He turned to the light switch in time to see the desk clerk's hand moving away from the switch. "You can't keep coming here and playing with the lights," she said.

Without regard for the clerk's words, Cam reached over and flipped the switch off. In the quick darkness, Cam couldn't see Susanna. He strained as much as he could, but there was no sign of her being there.

The clerk reached in again, turned the lights back on. She said, "I need to ask that you leave now!"

Cam could see that it was useless to try to say more. He knew two things could happen now. He hoped he had gotten through to Susanna to help. If not, she might vanish for good.

Cam met Katie down on the sidewalk outside the hotel entrance. He didn't have to say a thing to Katie. They both knew to run back to the church. On the way, he told Katie what took place.

Like Cam, Katie hoped he had said the right things.

BACK ON THE ROOF
Chapter 41

The one arm John had hooked through the strap of the backpack wasn't enough. He kept slipping more and more. He didn't think he could hold on much longer. He knew his only hope was in his friends doing something to help him.

"Help me," John yelled again. "Please."

"That's what I called out, over and over again, but no one came," the young ghost said.

"That is not true!" Susanna's voice echoed from behind Hamnet.

Hamnet stopped and turned towards her. John tried to see over the low point of the parapet. He could only see the back of Hamnet's ghostly figure.

"That is not true. I was there. I came and came, but no one would let me inside to see you . . ."

"That's a lie. You never came. I called for you, but you never came."

"I did come. Mother and Father forbade me to go to you. I was there. I did come. There was so much death all around. They were afraid for both of us."

Hamnet paused. The events he knew of that happened had faded through the years. Most of what he knew had been replaced by the visions of the men with the beastly faces. Then, he recalled something. "But you wrote about how your little brother died. You wanted all to know how grim and vile a death I had."

"No, I wrote to tell the world how brave you were. I wrote to tell the world that it was not your fault. I wrote to tell the world how horrid it was to die that way. I didn't want people to ever forget you. Father hadn't written about you, so it was up to me."

John waited to hear the next exchange between Hamnet and his sister, but nothing was said. John managed to pull himself up enough to take one last peek over the low wall. He saw them hugging. He felt his relief make his grip loosen. His time in the cold night had sapped most of his strength. He looked down to see where on the roof below he would hit before sliding off into the graveyard. It was as he looked down that he felt hands grab his arms. He looked up to see both the priest and Ruth holding on to him. The two of them were able to pull him up enough to where he could get a foothold. After that, he was able to get up and over the low wall. He fell to the floor, fully exhausted.

He looked up at his two rescuers. To him, they both looked like angels; the priest in his white robes, and Ruth, well, just looking like an angel to him.

Away from Danger

Chapter 42

It took John a few minutes before he could stand on his own. His legs and arms had no strength left in them. By the time the three got downstairs, Cam and Katie had arrived. Of course, the people who had been in the church had gathered to see what the fuss had been about. They cleared a path for John to sit down in the nearest pew. The priest asked an altar server to get a bottle of water for John. The water helped John regain some strength. The priest gave John about ten-minutes to rest before he asked him what he was doing hanging over the ledge.

John used his time to think of what to tell the priest. Like Katie, he didn't want to lie to a priest. Of course, he couldn't tell him he was arguing for his life with a ghost.

"I'm sorry, Father. I wanted some photos to post online that no one has posted before. I figured the best thing to do was sneak up to the roof. I could take some great photos from up there. The wind caught me by surprise and pushed me over the side. I guess God was watching over me and caught my backpack strap on the stones. Then, you all came. Believe me, it will never happen again."

The priest wasn't used to people lying to him, so he took John at his word about what happened. He was sure that John was up to no harm. He let John off easy and told him to never do that again.

While sitting on the pew, John opened the backpack and slid the box out. He opened the drawer. Sure that the papers were there, he slid the drawer shut and put the box back into his bag.

"Oh, my goodness," Ruth said. "I was so worried about you. Don't ever do anything like that again!" She gave him a long, tight hug, rocking back and forth.

"Don't worry. There's no way I'd do anything like that again," John said. He looked at Katie and Cam. "Thanks, I know you got to Susanna."

"No problem. Ruth filled us in. It's a good thing it worked out. It *did* work out, didn't it?" Katie asked.

"I'm alive and I've got the papers." A huge smile came across John's face. "I'd say, yes, it worked out. We can get those to Dr. Robins tomorrow."

"We'd better call your parents and let them know you're all alright. They will be worried about you, John. You've missed dinner!" Ruth said. She gave him a kiss. "I'm so happy you're alright."

"Yes, I think you're right about calling my parents." John looked down, his face turning a little red.

It turned out that John's parents were busy that night too. They had talked to the genealogist that day. They found out a lot about their bloodline there in Stratford. They found that they were linked to Hamnet Sadler. John's parents got on very well with the man. They were having dinner with him that night. They had tried leaving John a message. When John hadn't returned their call, they figured he was busy with Ruth and the others. His phone app showed he was at the church, so they felt they had nothing to worry about.

When he called them back, John kept his story brief. He just mentioned that he had been tracking a story he had found in a box he had bought. "I'll tell you all about it when I see you back at the hotel. Or if you're asleep, in the morning."

MEETING AT THE INSTITUTE
Chapter 43

John and Cam were both asleep by the time Tom and Jill returned to the hotel. The parents let the boys sleep. In the morning, John explained to his parents about the box, its hidden drawer, and the story. He left out the part of the ghost trying to kill him.

After breakfast, they all went to the Shakespeare Institute. John's parents as well as Ruth's dad also came along. John wanted them all to be there to hear it directly from Dr. Robins.

The girl who greeted them was a bit surprised. She wasn't used to having so many people outside her little window. She didn't have enough seats for them in the lobby. After some thought, she took them to the windowed room with the many chairs. The four friends noted it was the room from the other day. John and Ruth made sure to sit next to each other. This time, more staff members joined the group. The staff had heard from Dr. Robins about the papers. The news of the pages was too much to miss. They wanted to see them for themselves. It was quite a big deal for all involved.

Dr. Robins led the meeting. She said, "Thank you, so much for sharing this with us. We looked over the photos of the papers you shared. I was up most of the night looking them over. I couldn't believe what I was reading." Her face was beaming while she was saying that. "As you know, I told you I thought it was a story written by Susanna Hall. She was the Bard's oldest daughter. The Bard had three children, Susanna, and twins Hamnet and Judith. It was the death of Hamnet in 1596 that appears to be the subject of your papers."

John's parents were proud to hear how important something John found might be.

Dr. Robins went on, "At first, I told you it was a story. The more I looked it over, the more I found. Now, I'm thinking it might be an outline for a play. I suspect Susanna started to write a play about her brother. It is thought by some that he died of the plague. Here, Susanna starts her writing saying how brave her brother was in spite of his illness. I would guess she was trying to share her brother's story, but of course, we will need to see the other pages."

John knew first-hand what the story was about, but he couldn't tell Dr. Robins how he knew that. He knew she would find out for herself.

One of the others added, "Please know that at that time, women did not write these types of things. This will be the only known work of its kind from Shakespeare's daughter."

John knew it was time for him to pull the box out of his backpack. "Here is the box I bought in London. I know my girlfriend, Ruth, wanted to have it." He looked over to Ruth when he said that. He wasn't surprised to see Ruth blushing a little. Ruth certainly was happy with John's use of the word, girlfriend.

He placed the box on the table in front of him. Then, he moved two of the metal design pieces. The drawer slid open. John and his friends breathed a sigh of relief when the papers were there in the drawer. John was half thinking the ghost might have stolen the papers back. They all knew that the papers being there meant Hamnet was now at peace.

Dr. Robins held up a hand to stop John from picking up the papers. She brought out some thin cotton gloves and put them on. After that, she lifted the papers from the drawer with great care.

She spread the first five pages out on the table so the other staff members could see them. They all leaned in over the table to get a better look. They started asking John questions about where the box was found and how he found the drawer. They also asked what else was with the papers and many other questions. Detailed notes were taken on what was said.

John left the legal details about what to do with the papers up to his parents. They seemed happy to talk about that for him. John was glad to see they also kept Ruth's dad in the talk about who owned the papers. Their meeting didn't last as long as John had thought it would. In the end, Tom, Jill, and Kwame were sure that it would all be worked out.

The papers and the new found Sadler family history were all the talk at lunch. John could see there was a great friendship growing between his parents and Ruth's dad. He couldn't believe how well his mom's Christmas Market trip was ending. Before they came, he thought the trip would only offer shopping and some time with Ruth.

The friends headed back to John's hotel for the last time with the parents chatting quite a few yards behind. As they walked, they talked about some of the highlights of the trip. They thought they were far enough ahead and quiet enough that their talk was private from the parents. They were wrong. Somehow, John's dad overheard John mention ghosts.

"Ghosts? Did you just say ghosts? Did you feel the presence of a ghost, too? I felt something but didn't want to sound crazy by saying it might be a ghost. I mean, who believes in ghosts?"

The four tried their best to not laugh, and they almost did. John knew someday he'd have to tell his parents all about what really happened, but not quite yet.

LOOKING TO THE FUTURE
Chapter 44

The few days they had left in England were not as busy as the other days. And, like most trips, the last day came faster than they wanted. John and Ruth used whatever alone time they got to talk more openly about their relationship and where it was going. They used the word 'we' a lot.

Katie and Cam would travel back home on the same flight as the Sadlers. John was happy they would all be able to sit in the same row of the airplane though he wished Ruth would be coming too.

John's parents were looking forward to getting home. They got more than they expected from their trip. They were going home with new friends and family. Jill and Tom told Kwame and Ruth that they must visit them in the States. Kwame said they would. That gave John some hope of seeing Ruth again soon.

In Ruth's unique way of saying what she was thinking, she brought up a famous Shakespeare quote. "Parting is such sweet sorrow." John had heard that quote before, but now he truly understood its meaning.

For the four friends, it was like the end of summer school in Romania. It was hard for Cam and Katie to say goodbye to Ruth. Their hugs lasted a little longer than usual.

This goodbye touched Katie more than others in the past. Katie knew the three would be sharing their last semester of high school together. But after that, things would change. Cam thought about that too. She and Cam would go to college close to home.

John had taken his last days in England to tour Birmingham University with his parents and Ruth. He made up his mind to apply to go there after he finished high school. The people at the Institute implied that he'd have no trouble getting approved.

For John, saying goodbye to Ruth was so much harder than in Romania. He gave Ruth both a big hug and kiss, and said, "The time is going to go by so slowly. I don't want to say goodbye."

Ruth smiled and said, "It's only a 'see you later'."

THE END

Thank you for reading this story. Please consider giving it a rating/review at GoodReads, Amazon, or any site you normally leave reviews.

DISCUSSION QUESTIONS

1. Why do you think John was nervous to meet Ruth again?

2. How do you think John felt when he found out that his ancestors had lived in Stratford, England?

3. Would you ever think to buy something that seemed "spooky" to you? Do you believe there are such things as ghosts?

4. John and his friends had to find professional help to explain to them what they had found. What would you have done?

5. Near the end of the story, Katie and Cam talked to a ghost in order to save their friend. Do you think you could have the courage to talk to what you thought was a real ghost? How would you build up the courage to do that, if you did?

THE TRUE STORY

The town of Stratford-Upon-Avon was the home to the most famous author/playwright in the entire world, **William Shakespeare.** He was born there in 1564 and died there in 1616. He is known around the world as a playwright (one who writes plays), poet, and actor. His works (plays, poems, sonnets, and short poems) have been translated into more than 100 different languages. Some of his most famous plays were Romeo and Juliet, MacBeth, and Hamlet. These plays are still being performed today. (https://www.shakespearesglobe.com & https://facty.com)

His parents were John Shakespeare, an alderman (city councilman), bailiff (mayor), and glove maker; his mother was Mary Arden.

William Shakespeare married Anne Hathaway when he was 18 years old. Their marriage produced three children: Susanna, who was baptized at Holy Trinity Church on May 26, 1583, followed by twins, Hamnet and Judith, both baptized on February 2, 1585.

Shakespeare is commonly known as "The Bard." In his early and later years, the Bard lived in Stratford-Upon-Avon, while he spent the rest of his years in London. From about 1590 to 1613, Shakespeare lived mainly in London and by 1592 was a well-known actor there.

Hamnet Shakespeare was the son of William Shakespeare and Anne Hathaway, born in 1585 and died in 1596. Very little was ever written about Hamnet so not much is known about him. His actual date of death was never recorded, only the date of his burial. The cause of his death was never known. There were some theories that he might have died of the plague. However, the number of recorded deaths at that time do not show that plague was the likely cause, but it could have been. He had a fraternal twin sister, Judith, who lived to be 77 years old.

Shakespeare Institute - University Of Birmingham is located on Chapel street in Stratford-Upon-Avon. The Shakespeare Institute is a research institution that was started in 1951. Its goals are to expand the knowledge of Shakespeare studies and Renaissance drama. It works closely with the Royal Shakespeare Company, a drama group whose focus is the works of Shakespeare, which is also located in Stratford.

The institute offers postgraduate students a school where they can focus on subjects related to Shakespeare's works and Renaissance drama. The Institute offers both Masters and PhD degrees.

On their website, the Institute states: *The academic staff and research fellows are actively engaged in research on all aspects of Renaissance Drama, on the afterlife of Shakespeare in performance, on the culture of Renaissance England and on the impact of Shakespeare on modern culture.*

The Institute is funded in-part by the University of Birmingham.

Stratford-Upon-Avon tours. There are various tour companies that offer all sorts of tours of Shakespeare's home town. Some include ghost tours, as well as day tours. They are a great way to feel like you've seen Stratford and learned a lot about Shakespeare's life there.

I used one tour company while researching this book, Stratford Town Walk (https://stratfordtownwalk.co.uk/) and had a great time. It was a highlight of my visit to Stratford.

If you're looking for a fun and entertaining guide to Stratford, be sure to get a copy of Terry Deary's book, Horrible Histories: Stratford-Upon-Avon published by Scholastic.

PHOTO CREDITS:

Attribution: *Holy Trinity church, Stratford-Upon-Avon* by Philip Halling. Modified from original format https://commons.wikimedia.org/wiki/File:Holy_Trinity_church,_Stratford-Upon-Avon_-_geograph.org.uk_-_2303413.jpg

Chapter 4 Christmas Market
Chester Christmas Market, Northgate Street by Matt Harrop. Modified from original format https://commons.wikimedia.org/wiki/File:Chester_Christmas_Market,_Northgate_Street_-_geograph.org.uk_-_5603351.jpg

Chapter 5 Ruth's House and Her Dad
Photograph by Stephen McKay. Modified from original format.
https://commons.wikimedia.org/wiki/File:Ashley_Walk,_Mill_Hill_-_geograph.org.uk_-_458447.jpg

Chapter 9 Trinity Church
Holy Trinity Church, Stratford-upon-Avon by Paul Harrop. Modified from original format https://commons.wikimedia.org/wiki/File:Holy_Trinity_Church,_Stratford-upon-Avon_-_geograph.org.uk_-_4480216.jpg

Chapter 10 Train Ride to London
Photo by @cartroo on unsplash.com - Used with permission.

Chapter 26 Trinity Graveyard
Photo: Annan's old graveyard, Dumfries and Galloway by Rosser 1954. Modified from original format.
https://commons.wikimedia.org/wiki/File:Annan%27s_old_graveyard,_Dumfries_and_Galloway.jpg

AUTHOR BIO

R. Fulleman lives in Southern California and enjoys creating stories that entertain readers and introduce them to new places. He especially likes to encourage young readers and those new to reading English.

Other books in the series:

Faces in the Flames: A Ghost Story (Bk #1)

> Cam, a 14-year-old boy, travels to the South Pacific to scuba dive on the wreck of his grandfather's WWII ship. Cam and his dad are told not to enter the ship, nor take anything since it's considered a war grave.

A force calls Cam under the ship where a ghostly mystery starts to take over his life. With the help of his friends, Cam tries to stop the hauntings.

Heart of the Castle: A Ghost Story (Bk #2)

Katie didn't expect the most haunted castle in Europe to hold the answers to an incredible family secret. During a summer studying abroad in Transylvania, she finds herself at the gates of Bran Castle, the one-time prison of medieval ruler, Vlad "The Impaler." More recently, in life, Bran Castle was home to the King and Queen of Romania. In death, the castle was home to just the queen's heart.

Now, along with 15-year-old Katie's friends Cam, John, and new roommate Ruth, she uncovers a century-old mystery and a terrifying adventure. Will haunting spirits from the past lead her to safety and treasure, or push her into the hands of a deadly ex-secret policeman hunting for the same prize?